my beginning

my beginning

a novel

melissa kline

Lucky
PRESS

My Beginning

Published by:
Lucky Press, LLC, PO Box 754, Athens, OH 45701-0754
Email: books@luckypress.com SAN: 850-9697
Visit the publisher's website: www.LuckyPress.com
Visit the author's website: www.MelissaKlineAuthor.com
Purchase order fax: 614-413-2820 email: sales@luckypress.com
Book trailers: www.youtube.com/luckypressllc

ISBN: 978-0-9846317-5-9
Library of Congress Control Number: 2011927488

Author's photograph by Anissa Long Photography
(www.anissalongphotography.com)
Cover illustration and book design by Janice Phelps Williams
Cover texture by dreamstime.com / Adam Tomasik

PRINTED IN THE UNITED STATES OF AMERICA

Publisher's Cataloging-in-Publication

Kline, Melissa.

My beginning / Melissa Kline. -- Athens, OH : Lucky Press, c2011.
   p. ; cm.

   ISBN: 978-0-9846317-5-9
   Audience: ages 15 and up (grades 10 and up).

      1. Science fiction, American. 2. Interpersonal re-
   lations in adolescence--Fiction. 3. Dystopias--Fiction.
   4. Regression (Civilization)--Fiction. 5. Young adult
   fiction. 6. Bildungsromans. 7. Love stories. 8. Science
   fiction. 9. Alternative histories (Fiction) I. Title.

PS3611 .L5586 M9 2011   2011927488
813/.6--dc22   1107

✧ ✧ ✧

To my boys ~
Charles, Liam, Charles III and Pop

✧ ✧ ✧

confinement

They always made us wear bleached white aprons during meal preparation. I never understood why. Wouldn't the usual pleated navy jumper hide stains better?

I walked into the bright industrial kitchen gleaming with shiny stainless steel appliances and reflective countertops. Multiple workstations and islands filled the center of the room; while stoves, sinks, walk-in refrigerators, freezers and racks bordered the walls. The ceiling, or lack thereof, revealed exposed pipes and vents tangled together in a mess of function. I have always been intimidated by this room, feeling insignificant and unprepared.

The rest of the class hurried in from behind me eager to get started chopping, boiling and stirring, but I was hesitant.

Everyone had teams and partners picked out months in advance. Me, I was the odd one, always too quiet and shy to make many friends at all.

A mother nurse quickly rushed to my side.

"Ivory. Go join Alice and Kya."

I stared at the giggling girls who looked too much alike and not at all like me. Alice had olive skin dappled with freckles and curly light-brown hair. Kya's skin was a clear deep tan, complimenting her shiny ebony hair that appeared liquid when it moved.

I looked down at my pale, almost white skin, seeing blue veins that were eerily visible. I hated my skin. It was completely different from any of my brothers or sisters—at least from what I could see. The only vision I'd had of myself was a reflection in a pot of still water.

Mother nurse gently pushed my body toward the girls who were obviously not my blood sisters. They had just begun rolling out pastry dough, each one of them working hard to get the thickness perfect.

"Hi, Ivory." Alice flashed a fake smile in an attempt to be polite. "Here, you can cut this."

She dropped an unusually bright orange into my palm. I walked to the counter keeping distance from Kya and set the fruit onto an old wooden chopping block. The slab of wood was scarred from years of use. Without a word, Kya handed me a butcher knife and I broke the skin of the fruit. A spray of citrus erupted, awakening my senses.

Annoyed by my stalling, Kya grabbed the knife from me. "Just cut it...like this." She slammed the knife into the fruit creating two halves. "Now cut those into halves, and so on..."

I kept my eyes on the orange, trying not to overhear Kya and Alice mumbling insults about me, then quickly cut the halves as instructed and left the girls to their chatter. A small two-person table against the only available wall in the room was a rare sanctuary. I pulled the creaky wooden chair out, but a mother nurse appeared at my side.

"Ivory, what are you doing?"

"Is it alright if I sit out for today?"

"For what reason?"

"I'd like to observe the relationship between nurse and student." My carefully planned words came out in a flurry. "For research purposes."

Mother nurse gave my face a thorough examination. "Are you feeling unwell?"

"I am feeling very well." I lied.

Within seconds she had gone to a second mother nurse at the other side of the room. They congregated on my behalf, each of them staring me over at least once within the conversation. The second mother nurse finally walked to my table, handing me a notebook and pencil.

"Ivory, since you've decided not to participate, I want you to write a two-page descriptive essay on intervention skills as a mother nurse."

It could have been worse. "Alright."

"You are to sit quietly and not disturb anyone, understand?"

"Yes."

I watched her walk away in the standard grey button-down dress all of the mother nurses wore. She stood at the doorway, hands crossed, watching me with blank expression. I went to my notebook and scribbled in-between the blue lines before looking up again. I tried my best to keep my eyes on the nurses sprinkled throughout the kitchen, but I couldn't help but find the students much more interesting.

A group of three brothers were standing at a silver work-table near the ovens preparing chicken with vegetables. One of them had his white dress-shirt sleeves pushed up. He was sprinkling seasoning onto the meat, while another nearly burned his finger checking the oven. The third looked just as bored as I was, slowly chopping a line of freshly peeled carrots.

Another group, a trio of sisters including cruel Cassandra and her minion Emily, were too busy giggling to pay any attention to the lasagna noodles boiling over onto the stove.

A quick glance identified their distraction: Kyle was juggling eggs, Mason was doing a jig and Hammond's face was turning the same shade of red as the tomato sauce he was stirring.

"THAT'S ENOUGH!"

The crack of a pointing stick echoed throughout the room leaving nothing afterward but the sound of food boiling and sizzling. Kyle's eggs had fallen to the floor, and he was quickly removed from the class, leaving everyone unnerved.

I continued to scan the room and jotted down a few words, mostly for show. It wasn't until I reached a group on the far end of the kitchen that I was suddenly caught off guard.

Aidan was looking at me while he pressed round metal cutouts into pastry dough. When I met his unusual blue-grey eyes, he stopped. I quickly looked away, scribbling nonsense onto the paper, then waited for several minutes before daring to look back up. Aidan had gone back to his repetitive task, while his partners chuckled amongst themselves, reminding me of how rude Alice and Kya had been minutes earlier.

Aidan was the only one from the outside, sent to us from a different institution. He was never to speak of it and we were never to ask, but still my siblings hounded him with questions. Every one of the girls old enough to possess immodest feelings had a thing for Aidan since he was not a brother we'd grown up with. The fact that he was extremely attractive and eighteen only added to the appeal. Mother nurses had given many lashings since his arrival. Flirting or showing affection of any kind was forbidden.

When the bell finally buzzed, I had compiled nearly three pages of ridiculous writing. I was sure to turn it in to the mother nurse on the way out, getting a nod and half smile. We shuffled in lines up endless flights of stairs, then down a large plain white hallway to our rooms for an hour of peace—the best part of the day as far as I was concerned.

My first agenda was taking off the vile uniform I was forced to wear on a daily basis. I slipped the navy jumper off, unbuttoned the white cotton blouse underneath, then put on the grey pair of sweats used for sleeping in. The soft fabric embraced my skin. I crawled onto my small twin bed and released my hair from its tight bun. The wavy locks tumbled well past my shoulders as I grabbed a handful and stared at the straw-colored tresses. In my hand they were pretty, but what did they look like around my face?

"Hello, Ivory." Tessa walked in and set a stack of books on her set of drawers. "How was meal prep?"

"Dull." I disappeared under my blankets and took in a deep breath. I had just closed my eyes when the sound of obnoxious snickering filled the room.

"Poor Kyle. I hope he didn't get too punished." Cassandra's loud voice pierced my ears. "He was just being funny."

"Did you see Aidan?" Emily's voice squealed. "He seemed very interested in Ivory today. I saw him look at her *three* times in class."

"He was probably distracted by the glare coming off of her skin."

A fit of laughter shook the room.

"No one would ever be interested in *her*. She's too ugly."

"Be nice." Tessa attempted to defend me but it never worked.

"Did I tell you Paul wants to meet me in the east attic to talk?"

A dramatic gasp sounded. "No? When?"

I blocked out every sound in the windowless stark white room, going in my mind to another place as I always did. It was my only escape. I imagined a world filled with life, healthy life. A world just like the greenhouse, but natural, everything having a place and purpose. Vast expanses of gardens where water flowed crystal clear and animals from the past roamed the lands once again. I tried to imagine what birds would sound like in their natural song and what smells I might encounter. The smell of dirt like the potted plants and fruits I loved so much? I saw myself in this world, running free. I felt fresh air on my face as I ran through the thick greenery, happier than I had ever been. This feeling filled my heart with so much joy. *Freedom.* I dreamed of something I would never have. Not in this life.

A sudden jostle of my bed jolted me out of my fantasy.

"Ivory? Are you alright?" The soft voice of my one and only friend comforted me.

I turned to see Flora sitting on the edge of my bed looking concerned, her red ringlets wild around her face.

"Flora! I missed you." I sat up to face her, getting a chuckle.

"I just saw you this morning, silly."

"I know. I've just had a difficult day." I tugged at one of her curls.

"Why?"

I told her all about my meal preparation experience, then hinted to her about Cassandra and Emily being vicious again. Her freckled cheeks flushed. She turned to the three giggling girls all piled onto Cassandra's bed.

"Leave Ivory alone!" she yelled.

They appeared startled for a moment, then Cassandra's snake-like eyes squinted. "Or what?"

"Or I'll tell a mother nurse and you'll get lashings!"

"Big deal."

"You're going to get it!"

"I'll just tell them that I saw you touching a boy."

Flora looked like she was about to explode. "Fine! The next time you make fun of Ivory, I'll hit you myself!"

Cassandra laughed, causing her two minions to chortle right along with her.

"Flora." I whispered. "You don't have to do that."

"Oh, how I would love to hit that ugly evil face of hers."

I held back a laugh, scrambling for a different subject. "So, you're on tomatoes today, right?"

Her cheeks slowly returned to their usual rosy color. "Yes, tomatoes and squash."

"I've got garden thirteen."

"Well, we won't be too far apart." She cocked her head, causing her curls to bounce. "Do you have setting or kitchen duty today?"

"Kitchen duty."

"I have setting." Her gaze fell.

"But at assembly we both have choir."

"That's true." She grinned. "Maybe I can yell how my day was to you."

We chuckled the rest of the short hour away as I hurried to get re-dressed in proper uniform.

The third class of the day before lunch was communication studies, which I didn't mind so much. My desk sat near one of the many barred windows lining the room, allowing me to look out and daydream as always. Outside the massive brick building we called home the land looked fertile and lush, with overgrown plants and trees as far as my eyes could see. It didn't look dangerous or poisonous at all. To me, it seemed just the opposite.

From my seat facing south, I could barely see the roof of the infants' building where healthy babies were cared for and raised. I had been there once, though I was too young to remember it clearly.

The second separate building from the massive institution held the younger children, toddlers and up, until they were old enough to be of service. That was my favorite place. I had many happy memories of time spent with loving mother nurses who nurtured us into cheerful kids.

The big building where I had lived for six years now housed the oldest of us. Boys and girls were always separated into west and east wings, respectively. During the day, everyone gathered toward the center where floors of classrooms, gyms, kitchens, dining rooms, a spacious auditorium and huge greenhouse occupied all of our time. Day in and day out it was always the same, with the exception of the mother nurses mixing up our schedules and duties in an attempt to make things more exciting. They failed miserably. I dreamt of a day when it would once again be acceptable to step outside into the mystery of the world. The plague had made that impossible.

Throughout our entire lives we were never allowed to go outdoors, though I never understood why. The premise of our institution was clean and safe, the location chosen for that very reason. Besides that, routine inoculations kept us immune and protected—nobody had come down with the sickness for years. Still, they insisted on using the underground tunnel systems connecting each and every outside building, strictly used only by mother nurses and teachers.

The entire human race had come close to extinction, yet here I was, sixteen years old sitting in one of many safe havens still remaining for surviving children. Children were not allowed anywhere else, that's why I was here. We'd been prepared for a life of survival, knowing that once we matured we'd be sent as mother nurses and teachers to other institutions. Our lives had been mapped out for us, our destinies chosen. We were taught to be grateful and not to wish for things we could not have. There was no other option. If it were up to me, I'd take the risk of dying.

Lunch was repetitive: meet Flora, stand in line for food, get food, sit as far away from everyone else as possible, eat. I had grown so tired of the same menu with the same foods offered over and over again; my diet consisted only of fruit and an occasional vegetable. Every once in a while I'd eat a chicken breast to keep my strength up, but everything else was revolting. Flora had grown accustomed to finishing off my plate as well as hers.

"Ivory, you really should eat more." Flora advised, taking a bite of corn. "You're too thin. The mother nurses are going to think you're getting sick."

"Maybe that's why they've been testing me weekly."

Flora nodded. "Here..." She shoved my plate back in front of me. "Eat."

I poked the half eaten food with a fork, lost in thought. "Don't you ever wonder what it's like beyond this place?"

Flora's eyes widened. She leaned over in a whisper. "Don't talk about that here."

"Why is it so terrible? Why should I be punished for having questions?" I stabbed my fork into the meatloaf, the frustration of the unknown building. I wondered where the beef for the meatloaf came from, thinking that if the plague was still deadly, there wouldn't be cows. I questioned where our clothes came from, where the utensils came from, how we managed to have clean running water, how new books and supplies just appeared. I wasn't sure when I started questioning everything, but somehow it just didn't add up. The worst part about my questioning was that it was forbidden. Any information that was not handed to us was off limits. The best I could do was hope that someday I would know all of the answers. Meanwhile, I went mad with skepticism.

A sudden bump of the table to my left got my attention as a banana fell in front of me. I looked up to see Aidan holding a tray with a silly smile, his clean-cut light brown hair disheveled.

"Sorry." He looked into my eyes. "You can have that if you want."

I immediately tensed. "Thanks."

Flora looked at me with wide eyes, then we burst into laughter, trying not to get too out of control. I concentrated on peeling the yellow skin of the banana, taking a hearty bite.

"It was nice of him to give it to you," Flora commented.

"Yes, it was."

Thoughts of Cassandra's hurtful words drifted back into my mind, piercing my heart.

"Flora? Am I ugly?" I asked.

She frowned at me, looking angry again. "Is that what Cassandra said?"

I nodded.

Flora grunted, her eyes peering down at the table. After a

few seconds of hateful glaring, she turned back to me.

"Ivory, I've told you before, you're beautiful. Why don't you believe me?"

"Because when I look down at myself I see ugly, and Cassandra always tells me I'm ugly. I don't look anything like anyone else."

"You know who's ugly?" she asked, her tone very serious. "Cassandra. She's the definition of ugly. She only wishes she could look like you."

My lips curved. "I wish I looked like you. I love the color of your hair and your freckles."

She wrinkled her nose. "I'd rather have skin like yours, fair and clear. And your eyes are the prettiest sky blue. It's no wonder Aidan dropped his banana."

We ended up in a fit of laughter again, the way we always did.

❖ ❖ ❖

Plague sciences, nurse economics and institutional engineering were incessantly slow, especially since I was looking forward to working in the greenhouse.

I rushed back to my room after the last afternoon class and quickly changed slipping on a pair of navy blue slacks. I tucked the short-sleeved white blouse into them, then hurried toward the front entrance. On my way through the huge wooden double doors—once the main passage into the building—I grabbed a gardening apron and threw it on over my head, taking in a deep breath of earth.

The habitat was like an indoor backyard, completely sealed and attached like any other room. There were a variety of trees, plants, fruits, vegetables, flowers and bushes—each and every one of them having a zone and special area according to lighting, temperature and compatibility. Little walkways divided the zones, making everything easily accessible. It was always humid and warm smelling of soil and flowers. To me, the smell was intoxicating.

A few of my siblings were already at work tending to their gardens. I took a quick look toward the tomatoes for Flora. Kya was checking the soil, but there were no red curls to be found. I made my way to garden thirteen, which had strawberries, beans, lettuce, borage, onions, spinach, marigold and a variety of spices. It was a large garden that kept me busy watering and maintaining for most of the hour. I grabbed a watering can and crouched to the ground, getting close and personal with the foliage. Every once in a while I'd press my fingers into the dirt, feeling the damp cool texture on my skin. I loved everything about it—the way it felt on my hands, the way it looked on my skin. I'd even dreamt of rolling around in the gardens, a fond fantasy that always made me giggle.

A quiet whisper got my attention back toward the tomatoes where Flora was donning a dirty apron and giving me a big smile. She waved and I waved back, looking only for a minute before going back to my infatuation.

After the daily tasks of the facility had been tended to, everyone prepared for supper by getting cleaned up and changed as necessary. Those who had longer chores stayed wherever they were needed, while others prepared dinner and the dining area. Flora and I always seemed to have different assignments when it came to supper. Kitchen duty was the more difficult of the two, which was the one I always had. It was starting to get old.

Once again, I wasn't very hungry, and by the time assembly came around I was feeling lightheaded. Assembly was held in the auditorium every evening after supper. It was always two hours of announcements, singing and quiet reflection. My favorite was the quiet. I wondered if I would make it through the ceremony or if anyone would notice me not really using my voice in the choir.

I saved some energy by not singing every single note, but somehow all of that seemed insignificant after I locked eyes with Aidan. At first I thought I was just imagining it and I tried my hardest not to look again. Of course, my eyes deceived me by drifting toward the left side of the audience where we exchanged glances. My cheeks burned with heat. I hoped no one would guess the unusual feelings going on inside of me. I was suddenly painfully aware of every blink, breath and petty movement. My heart raced, threatening to explode in my chest. An overwhelming dizziness washed over me as I quickly composed myself, thinking it would be mortifying to have to be carried off the stage. I concentrated as hard as I could on the musical notes, actually using my voice this time, and didn't dare look his way again.

That night, as I lay cloaked in covers, my mind went back to Aidan and the astonishing effect he'd had on me. I had never experienced anything like it and couldn't decide whether I hated it or liked it. I had even considered the fact that maybe I really was getting sick and it had nothing to do with him. Was I truly going insane? I wondered why he would even look at me in the first place. Was it because I was strange like Cassandra always reminded me, or could it have been something else? I knew there was no way any boy would ever be interested in me, even if such an interest was allowed. I concluded that it had to be something else. I also decided right then and there that I would ignore completely and forget about the odd spell he'd cast over me. There was no way I was ever going to let that happen again. Ever.

proximity

I failed miserably.

I wasn't sure how, but within the course of a week Aidan and I had started a game. He looked at me, I looked at him. I looked at him, he looked at me. It was addictive. The more I told myself not to, the worse it got. Luckily, no one, not even Flora, had noticed. We'd both been careful to keep it as confidential as possible.

And, I was wrong. It wasn't just a sickness or that I was going insane. Well, maybe I was going insane, but I had confirmed that my "episodes" really were because of him. Every glance sent me into another spin that left me feeling lightheaded. I told myself that it was harmless and didn't mean a thing, that it was merely a distraction from our ordinary dull lives. It gave new meaning to everything, making my days a lot more exciting and bearable.

After a delightfully flustering meal preparation class, I fled up the basement steps with a burst of giddy energy. My head was somewhere in the clouds as crowds of children eager to get back to their rooms rushed past me, completely unaware of my delusion. I stopped on the second landing, looking out at the world unknown to me through the tall thick-paned window and its bars. Rain pelted the glass, making it difficult to see, but still I stood in wonder trying to imagine what the rain might feel like on my skin. I had managed to block out the sound of commotion and footsteps scurrying by when a presence behind my right shoulder caught my attention. I stood completely still, unsure of who it was.

"Do you want to get out of here as bad as I do?"

My heart skipped a few beats recognizing the newly memorized voice. I turned to see Aidan with curiosity in his eyes looking just as intrigued by the rain as I was. Within seconds he was gone as a mother nurse stepped onto the landing.

"Ivory, quit dawdling. Up to your room, now."

"Yes, mother nurse."

Over and over again his soft voice and the words spoken played in my mind, interfering with my concentration during the rest of the day. Flora had even asked what was wrong with me during break and lunch. I kept to myself as much as I could, never again looking his way.

The next day, I got a frown of concern from him during meal prep, instantly setting my stomach into flutters. He looked worried, as if afraid that what he had said upset me. With a sigh, I went back to the raw chicken I was slowly rolling in breadcrumbs. I wished I could have a normal conversation with him, but that was impossible.

I stared into the bowl, coating one of the last pieces of meat, when a spark of creativity hit me. My eyes shifted around the room, making note of where each and every mother nurse stood. I glanced to my right seeing Alice absorbed in potatoes and Kya kneading a ball of dough. Nobody was even remotely interested in my presence.

I threw the meat onto a large cookie sheet with the rest of the pieces then strategically sifted breadcrumbs through my fingers onto the metal. After checking my surroundings once more, I headed to the ovens with the flat pan steady in both hands hoping that nobody, other than the one person I wanted to, noticed it.

Aidan stood at the stove right next to the oven looking a little apprehensive. Somehow he knew I was up to something. I walked straight toward him, opened the cold oven and shoved the pan at him. I pretended to merely double check my meat, lingering for just a second. Without looking up, I knew he saw the letters Y-E-S spelled out with breadcrumbs. I jerked the pan toward the oven, purposely shaking the letters into a frenzy.

"Ivory, what are you doing?" Alice came up from behind me looking annoyed. "I thought we weren't ready to cook those yet?"

"I was just going to get them started." I snapped the oven to preheat for effect.

She took a glance at the pan then shot me a cynical look. "That's really messy. You should shake some of those bread crumbs off or they'll burn."

"Alright." I pursed my lips, holding back a laugh.

◇ ◇ ◇

The stairwell became a meeting place of sorts, where every day I would casually stop to look out the window and every day Aidan would stop to either answer or ask a question. We would never look to each other or act like we even knew one or the other was around; I would simply just stare out the window and speak one or two words.

The day of my crumb creation, I had boldly asked why he looked at me. It wasn't until the next day that he answered, saying that he found me intriguing. This got to me. Intriguing? Like amusing…entertaining…funny? Like a clown?

That night I tossed and turned, eager to know why. I had asked and was waiting for my answer, hoping it would come soon. The one-sentence conversations were killing me, getting more and more frustrating with each day.

Crystal clear water stretched before me cradled by earth and rock. My hands created circular patterns that spiraled and rippled in an endless rhythm. Every inch of water was affected. A feeling of happiness surrounded me -- until I was aware of my body. My legs began to feel cold on the hard rocky shore and I realized I was naked. I stood and walked slowly into the water allowing the cold to envelop me until I was completely submerged. A reflection of myself stared back at me in a glossy mirror. Words of desperation escaped my lungs but no one could hear me. I was trapped….

"Ivory! Be quiet!"

I sat up in a state of terror with a terrible feeling in the pit of my stomach. My hands and feet were numb with cold and my eyes were completely blind. For a second I wondered where I was, then reality came sinking back in. I shivered into my blankets, wishing I could at least see something other than darkness to sidetrack the horrible feeling. My heart eventually calmed to a reasonable pace when a sudden beam of light hit my face. I squinted toward the door to see Cassandra coming in. The light disappeared as she shut the door, then the sound of shuffling and her bed squeaking filled the silent room.

"Emily? Are you awake?" Cassandra whispered.

"Yes, thanks to Ghost."

"I met him."

"You did? What did you do?"

"We talked and he told me he wants to meet again."

Emily gasped.

I covered my head with my pillow and curled up into a ball when light flooded the room. A raging mad mother nurse stood in the doorway.

"Come with me," she instructed, glaring at Cassandra whose face had lost all color. I watched her walk out the door and into the hall, then the mother nurse turned the lights off with her special key and it was black again. The silence was eerily daunting. My thoughts went to my roommate, wondering just how bad her punishment would be.

I awoke to the same routine bell that startled me every morning. Aidan drifted through my mind while I quickly got dressed and headed to the adjacent girls bathroom. Sleepy eyed girls littered the sinks and stalls as I found my way to an empty basin and splashed my face with water. I let my hair down and raked water through the strands before winding the curls back into a proper bun. Waves temporarily sprung to life, but only for minutes. Even my hair was confined.

I returned to my room to find an image that was terrifying. Cassandra's raw and beaten back was exposed, covered with thick swollen red lines. She had been lashed bare at least ten times with a pointing stick. I swallowed hard, feeling bad for her and a little scared for myself. There was no way my thin body could ever handle such a thing.

Aidan kept his eyes locked on the uninteresting pasta dish he, Peter and Charlie were making. I tried everything, from creating lots of unnecessary noise, to "accidentally" spilling things. I had even stood right in front of him at one point within the class, being a little too courageous. He never once looked up. Needless to say, I was irritated. I stomped up the stairs, stopped at the window and waited. Nothing. A mother nurse eventually scolded me, setting the pace for the rest of the miserable day.

✧ ✧ ✧

Three days. I waited three excruciatingly long days with absolutely no eye contact or recognition. Aidan had been completely ignoring me, purposely ignoring me, which was worse than just not being noticed. He was consciously wiping me out of his life. I was upset and decided I had to do something.

On the fourth day, during greenhouse duty, I noticed him working amongst the Japanese cherry trees. I left my garden, not thinking very rationally, and deliberately walked to his supply cart. He was deep in concentration reaching up into the blossoming trees.

"What is wrong with you?" I asked. He turned with shocked expression, suddenly looking paranoid.

"Go back to your garden," he ordered.

"No."

He looked at me as if I were insane, then turned back to the tree.

I grabbed a spade from the cart and walked to the tree right beside his. "Why are you ignoring me?"

He didn't bother to look. "I have to."

"Why?"

"I don't want you to get hurt."

My heart fluttered as words were lost. Light pink petals flitted in front of me, eventually hitting the ground. I quickly remembered that he owed me an answer, suddenly needing it terribly.

"I'm 'intriguing'?" I asked, unconsciously scanning his muscular arms suspended in the tree. He stopped for a second then turned to look me deep in the eyes. My body began its routine reaction of sending my heart racing.

"You're the most beautiful thing I've ever seen." He paused to look up at the pink puffs. "Besides these trees." A smile curved his lips turning my brain to mush. I was sure I would faint.

"Ivory? Why aren't you in your garden?" It took me a second to register one of the nicer mother nurses standing beside the cart.

"I was just admiring the blooms." I smiled up into the tree. "And I misplaced my spade, so Aidan let me borrow his."

"Oh, alright. Well, get back to work please."

Walking away from him was one of the hardest things I've ever done.

◇ ◇ ◇

Two days passed without any interaction between us, yet I was still on a high, never coming down from the sweetest words that had ever been spoken to me. I drifted through the days in a trance performing my duties with a sudden optimism that apparently hadn't gone unnoticed.

During the usual early morning bathroom routine, I had just finished creating my bun, spending a little extra time making sure it was perfect. I pulled a tendril loose and curled it around my finger when Cassandra and Emily's words caught my attention. I glanced down the line of benches to see them watching me, snickering as they brushed their hair.

"...she's been acting strange."

"I think she likes a boy."

My stomach churned.

"I wonder who it is?"

"Probably Smelly Seth."

They giggled at themselves thinking they were funny.

"It's too bad. Nobody will ever like her, not even Smelly Seth."

A surge of anger shot through me. I stood, contemplating slapping Cassandra right in the face, but instead walked past them. I was about to head out the door but Emily stopped me. "I'm going to ask Aidan to meet me."

"You are?"

"Yes. He sits right next to me in communication studies, so it'll be easy."

My heart sank, though I wasn't sure why.

I struggled to concentrate all through my first class, wondering if something had changed between Aidan and me. The fact that he'd still been ignoring me the past couple days didn't help at all. It didn't occur to me how much it all meant, how much he meant, until that very moment. I was getting attached.

After helping Kya slice what seemed to be hundreds of tomatoes, she informed me that we needed a deeper pan and sent me to go find one. I walked past workstation after workstation; my nose getting bombarded with new smells every couple of feet. I was sure to note that Aidan was standing near the refrigerator holding a clear container of mushrooms. He disappeared inside the cold room as I walked toward it on my way to a storage space near the stoves. I passed a cold draft escaping from the door, keeping my eyes glued forward, when a sudden yank at my apron sent me into shock. I found myself standing inside the refrigerator staring into Aidan's smiling eyes.

"You scared me," I breathed.

"I'm sorry."

I hoped the cold would dampen the heat burning on my cheeks and all through my body. Being only a few inches away from him did magical things to me.

"Will you meet me somewhere?" he asked.

I didn't even need to think. "Yes."

"Wait a half hour into period three, then be excused to the restroom and meet me in the second-floor broom closet, right next to the girls bathroom."

I was flattered. He'd obviously put some thought into it. "Alright."

It wasn't difficult at all simply "going to the bathroom," and the broom closet door was literally inches away from the bathroom door, making it easy. I slipped into the closet, my insides doing flips seeing Aidan's perfect face in the dim light. All of a sudden we were in a quiet musty smelling box all by ourselves. It was the first time I'd ever been alone with anyone -- other than a mother nurse.

We stood in an awkward silence standing only a couple feet away. I was trembling with nerves.

"Well...," I broke the silence, needing to hear my own voice, "this is..."

"Sterile?" He raised an eyebrow giving a smile.

I looked at all of the bright cleaners neatly lined up on the shelves along with disposable towels and dusting materials. Then a gathering of dirty mops propped up in the corner caught my eye.

"Not really."

We burst into laughter chasing away some of the uneasiness.

"It's sort of strange, isn't it?" he asked, his eyes examining my face. "To finally be able to say whatever we want after trying for days just to have a conversation."

"I don't know what to say."

"I don't either."

We smiled at each other.

"That bread crumb thing was pretty crafty."

I smirked. "You did see it."

"But it wasn't half as amusing as the day you spilled gravy—twice."

I frowned. "You're stubborn."

"I'm trying not to get us caught." He smiled, making my heart melt. "The garden incident is by far my favorite though."

I grinned, agreeing silently. "Did you really mean what you said?"

"Yes." He looked a little flustered. "Aren't you going to ask me about where I came from and what it was like?"

I smiled into his eyes. "Maybe another day."

That first conversation was the beginning of many more. At first we would meet only a few times a week, testing out the times and days that were safest, but it quickly grew into an every day routine. Together we'd figured out a system that was foolproof, making our chances of getting caught slim.

He was like a drug and I was addicted. Everything about him was perfect. He was smart, sweet, funny and always polite, never failing to make me feel special.

We'd gotten comfortable with each other, talking about all kinds of different subjects including our skepticism regarding what we'd been taught about the state of the world. Some days we laughed, sometimes we had deep captivating conversations, but no matter what, we always enjoyed our time together. Every second was precious.

I'd begun to keep a mental list of what to talk about with Aidan and what I wanted to ask, though there never seemed to be enough time. Fifteen minutes was average, twenty was stretching it and a few times we'd pushed it to nearly a half hour. We'd start talking immediately and ramble as fast as we could, taking advantage of every second.

As always, getting out of class was not a problem. I walked with a normal pace down the barren hall, keeping my eyes out for any lingering mother nurses. When it was safe, I quickly snuck into the empty closet and shut the door behind me. I shifted some boxes to create a seat for myself, then sat waiting. Thoughts of the first embarrassing question I wanted to ask turned my stomach into knots.

The door opened and Aidan appeared, closing the door behind him. He turned to me with a smile, his grey eyes gleaming.

"Hello."

"Hi." I glanced at the wall behind him. "Have you talked to Emily?"

"No, I ignore her. Why?"

"I think she wants to meet with you."

His focus went to the floor. "I wouldn't risk meeting anyone other than you. It's not worth it."

"I feel the same," I said, smiling.

"But we can never get caught," he said, meeting my gaze. "It would be terrible."

"I know."

"Have you ever met Oliver?"

"No. Nobody has."

"I have."

My eyes widened. "You have? When?"

"When I first arrived. He wanted to meet and welcome

me," Aidan said. A whole round of new questions swirled in my head.

Oliver Driscoll was the elusive head of the institute. There had been rumors that he wasn't a very nice person, which always made me wonder why he would be in charge of a children's institution.

"What was he like?"

"He seemed nice enough. I met him in the library of his mansion. He stood from his desk to shake my hand, and told me he hoped I enjoyed it here, that was about it."

"What did he look like?"

"He was clean-cut, wearing a suit. A little taller than me with dark hair."

"I can't believe you met him."

"Why not?"

"Nobody's even seen him."

"I can see his mansion from the west wing, through certain windows."

"Really?"

Aidan nodded.

"What was your other institution like?"

He grinned. "I thought you'd never ask."

My cheeks blazed at the realization that he was thinking about me as much as I was him.

"It was very similar to this one, only the building was a little different. There were mother nurses and teachers, classes—all the same schedules and routines."

"And that's where you grew up?"

"Yes."

"Why did they move you?"

He looked down. "The plague."

My heart sank.

"It killed all of them," Aidan said.

Silence engulfed the tiny room.

"I'm so sorry," I offered, suddenly tortured with emotion at the thought of what he must have seen. "I'm glad you survived."

He smiled, but a hint of sadness still traced his eyes. "I don't feel like I belong here, Ivory. I've always felt different from everyone else."

I smirked. "You're not the only one. I look like a ghost."

He gazed at me. "You look like a goddess."

Butterflies fluttered throughout my stomach.

"Can I see your hair?"

I waited a minute then pulled the pins from my bun, causing the golden locks to spill down my back. Aidan stared at me in awe, making me a lot more than a little self-conscious. I tried to control my feelings, thinking of what I wanted from him.

"Can I touch your hand?" I asked.

Without hesitation he held his hand up, palm facing out. I inched my own hand up to his, amazed by the warmth and sensation it created. I was fascinated and overwhelmed by the unfamiliar experience.

"I've never touched another human being. Not on purpose." I said, still struck by his warm skin.

"I haven't either."

"When I was little the mother nurses used to hold me. I miss that."

I traced the lines and muscle of his palm with my fingers, then he captured my hand in his, interlocking our fingers. My body's reaction to his touch was a hundred times more intense than what his eyes did to me. Sensations that were completely new stirred rapidly inside. I quickly pulled away, surprised and a little ashamed by my feelings. Unsure of what to do next, I swiftly pulled my hair into a ponytail and wound it back to its formal place.

"We should probably get going," he said, looking a little apprehensive.

I nodded, set the last pin in place, then jumped off the boxes. "See you tomorrow?"

"Tomorrow." He gave me a sweet smile before I slipped back into the hallway. I dreaded going back to class.

escape

Just for good measure, Aidan and I stopped meeting for nearly a week. A patrolling mother nurse had inhibited our ability to get together more than once. That week was excruciating. My heart ached to see his beautiful eyes and hear the comforting sound of his voice. I missed his laughter, our engaging conversations and the feel of his intoxicating energy. I spent my time, day and night, dreaming about his touch, imagining what his fingers might feel like on my face or in my hair. I envisioned him holding me in the small confines of the closet, wondering what feelings that would awaken. All I knew was that I had to be close to him, even if it meant getting caught. I was desperate to see the boy I had fallen madly in love with.

While exiting meal prep on a particularly draining day, Aidan's soft breath tingled my ear. He whispered for me to meet him fifteen minutes into period four. My heart danced away, unrestrained in its desire. The lack of sleep from my fantasy filled night no longer affected me.

During rest hour, I didn't hear Cassandra's snide remarks when she and Emily left the room, and I barely registered Tessa announce she was going to the greenhouse. I was too busy staring up at the colorless ceiling, though I wasn't seeing anything at all. My mind was hard at work contemplating whether or not to tell Aidan about my feelings. I wondered if it would be such a good idea at all, then I worried whether or not he felt the same. A frown creased my brow, then the door opened, scrambling my thoughts.

"Hi, Ivory." Flora walked in and sat on the edge of my bed.

I sat up, pulling my legs underneath me. "Hi."

She stared at me, her face twisted with worry. "Won't you tell me what's going on?"

My gut sank with guilt. I'd been evading her questions and concerns for too long.

"Ivory?"

"You can't speak a word of it, to *anyone*."

"I won't," she promised, truly sincere. Flora was the only person, besides Aidan, that I knew I could trust.

"I've been meeting someone."

"A boy?"

"Yes."

"I knew it." She looked to me with concern. "Ivory, I don't think that's such a good idea."

"It's alright. We've got it all figured out."

"We?" she asked. "Who is he?"

I hesitated.

"You can tell me, if you want."

"Aidan."

Flora gasped, her eyes wide with wonder. She took a minute to think it over. "You have feelings for him, don't you?"

I nodded.

"Ivory, that is so dangerous. What if you get caught?"

"I won't."

"Don't you remember what happened to Annette?"

I nodded, thinking about the girl who had supposedly done a lot more than just talking with a boy named Drake. After being caught they were both sent away, never to be seen again.

"Who knows what happened to her?"

"That's not going to happen to me, alright?"

She looked away, clearly troubled. "Well, you should at least start acting a little more...unhappy."

I chuckled.

"Really, you act completely different. Someone is bound to notice."

"I told you, we're taking precautions."

"That doesn't make me feel any better. I don't want to lose my most special friend."

Tears came to my eyes. "It's alright, Flora. You're not going to lose me."

❖ ❖ ❖

To my surprise, the closet had been rearranged and filled with even more boxes, making it nearly impossible to move around in there. I stood in the only available square left in the room wondering how Aidan and I were going to have a comfortable conversation. He walked in, barely able to shut the door as I squeezed as far as I could toward the boxes. We stood face to face, literally inches away. Every part of me was alert to him as we stared into each other's eyes.

"Maybe we should try the other closet, next to the boys' bathroom?" I offered.

He stared at me with intense eyes. "Maybe."

I swallowed, my mind drunk with an unmistakable desire. I fought the overwhelming urge to let my body fall into his.

"Ivory." He touched my hand, gently wrapping his around it. "I don't know what love feels like, but I think I feel it with you."

My heart fluttered beneath my chest as I released myself, allowing us to come into full contact. I rested my head just underneath his chin feeling his arms wrap tightly around me. An overwhelming wave of love washed over my entire being sending me into a euphoric state. I closed my eyes to memorize the sensation of our loving embrace, never wanting to be anywhere else.

"You're not upset?" he asked, his voice laced with relief.

I smiled up at him. "I'm very upset." I grinned. "That you didn't tell me about this earlier."

He beamed at me, grazing his nose tenderly against mine. I nuzzled my face into his while he released my hair, tangling his fingers into the curls. My hands searched his strong back and shoulders seeming tiny and frail in comparison. We stood in our two-foot square lovingly holding and caressing each other, relishing the newness of it all. Our time together was up way too soon, though it had been at least half an hour. I seriously contemplated never leaving.

Our passion grew beyond anything I could have ever imagined. I was completely and totally in love. I lived for our fleeting minutes in the closet where we could freely express our feelings for each other in such a natural and tender way. Everything about us felt right. I couldn't imagine ever getting punished for what seemed to be such a pure, harmless thing. I didn't understand why loving him was so wrong.

I had begun to notice one particular mother nurse keeping a watchful eye on me. She followed me to a few of my classes, made sure I was in my room when I was supposed to be, and even started trailing behind me between meals, chores and assembly. I was starting to get a little paranoid, though I hadn't said a thing to Aidan about it. My desire to be with him was far greater than any rational reasoning or common sense.

On a particularly bright sunny day, I awoke feeling refreshed and energized. First period had gone well and I made it a point between classes to stand in the warm radiant light beaming through the windows. The feel of the sun on my face was indescribable and had always been one of my favorite things. I couldn't help but imagine what it would feel like with Aidan by my side.

My scout of a mother nurse happened to be on duty during meal prep, so I made sure to never look in Aidan's direction. I thought I was doing well, and by the time Kya, Alice and I had just about finished with our casserole, I was no longer worried. I went about my business being cooperative and even a little cheery, when a couple of dramatic gasps sounded from the opposite side of the room. I looked to see Aidan clutching his fingers, noticing blood dripping from his hand. Out of pure instinct I leapt to his side and gently held his fists.

"Are you alright? How bad is it?"

The look on his face made me realize what I was doing. I immediately dropped my hands and backed away, feeling multiple probing eyes on me. A mother nurse rushed to his side and led him out of the room. I stood, immobile.

"Ivory?" My nemesis summoned me out to the hall, causing my stomach to twist. She bore a hole in my head as I tried desperately not to make eye contact. "You are *never* to touch a boy. Is that clear?"

"Yes, mother nurse. I'm sorry. I was just—"

"*Never*, for any reason at all."

"I understand."

"Do you understand that you have just set a bad example for your siblings?"

I struggled with the word. "Yes."

"Get back to work."

I worried terribly when Aidan never came back to class and resisted the urge to go to the clinic to peek in on him. After my stunt during meal prep, I knew it would be way too risky. We had previously planned to meet during third period that day, and I couldn't help but fret over whether or not it was still safe for us to meet. My intuition told me that it was probably not a good idea, but I couldn't bear the thought of his attempt to see me when I wasn't there.

During communication studies, my escape wasn't so easy. I raced to finish a paper, getting a strange look from the teacher, then finally got the pass and hurried toward the closet door. I reached for the knob when a pair of bony fingers dug into my arm. I was yanked with such force I lost balance.

"Come with me." The mother nurse who had been plotting my demise dragged me down the hall, walking so fast I could barely keep up. Her hand inflicted pain and I started to panic. My heart raced a million beats per second as I feared the unknown. I was scared to death, but not because of the pain I would most likely encounter or the possible isolation.

I was afraid that I would never see Aidan again. My eyes began to well with tears.

"IVORY!" His panicked voice shot through my ears. I struggled to see him far down the hall, being restrained and dragged away by a male teacher.

"Ivory! Let her go!" he yelled, causing my tears to flow freely. I tried with all of my strength to free myself from the clutches of the woman yanking me along, but she dug in even harder, throwing my body forward. The painful realization that it was the end for us broke my heart, sending me crying into uncontrollable sobs. We turned the corner as I glanced one last time down the long hallway, seeing Aidan still struggling and causing commotion. The mother nurse heaved me down flights of stairs until we reached a cold, dark basement. The hallway was endless with nothing but light after light, revealing doors for storage and unused rooms. We reached a door with a small mesh screened window where the mother nurse stopped and took out her set of keys. She unlocked the door then threw me into cold darkness.

The flicker of buzzing lights lit up a medium-sized room with ugly light-grey walls. A single cot covered in a white sheet was shoved in one of the corners with a shiny medical tray sitting nearby. A box of disposable gloves sat on top of the tray and a small trash can stood a few inches away. I looked to the woman holding a long black pointing stick, trembling with fear.

"Remove your clothes," she instructed, her face blank.

I shook my head, shaking uncontrollably. Before I could blink, she had unzipped my jumper and tugged it down. I watched it fall to the floor as she ripped open my blouse, causing tiny white buttons to scatter on the cement. She yanked my underclothes off and I stood in nothing but my shoes and knee-high socks. I hunched in the cold, attempting to cover myself.

"Lie on the bed."

Completely vulnerable and with no other options, I complied, lying stiff on the cot. I was completely exposed, terrified and embarrassed. The mother nurse set her weapon aside, then walked to the cot and analyzed my body with her eyes. She heaved me back and forth, carefully inspecting every inch of me. I could have sworn it was over until she gave me a physical examination. I felt a like a science experiment as I squirmed beneath her, crying out in protest. She finally took her hands off of me and walked back to her stick.

"Get up," she ordered.

Feeling violated, I slowly sat up and stood, never moving away from the bed.

She nodded toward the rusty drain in the middle of the floor that I gradually sidled to.

"Turn and face the wall."

I swallowed hard and faced the blank slab of grey. My eyes focused on a small dot, then a sudden searing pain shot throughout my entire body. I collapsed to the floor.

"Get up."

My back stung with such intensity I could barely breathe. I sobbed, knowing I couldn't handle much more.

"Please," I begged.

"The punishment for misbehaving with a boy is ten lashes—you shall get fifteen. Now, get up!"

I tried to stand but my muscles were weak, threatening to give out. Another crack and I screamed out in pain falling completely to the floor. I flinched, curling up into a tight ball. A loud repetitive alarm sounded.

The sirens.

I looked up to see the mother nurse drop her arm, startled and completely caught off guard. She stared down at me one last time before heading for the door. I watched her disappear, then quickly sat up grabbing every piece of strewn clothing. I began to dress as swiftly as possible despite the damaged articles. Being back in the torn uniform created a small sense of normalcy, making me feel just a little bit better. With a tiny burst of hope I went to the door and turned the knob, but it was locked. I pounded on the window, shook the knob a few more times, then gave up, sitting in the corner opposite the bed. With the cold cement pressed to my back I tucked my legs in, hugging them close. All I could think of was Aidan, and I began to cry. Horrible pictures flashed through my mind of him in the west wing basement getting tortured just as badly, if not worse, than I was.

The sirens screamed in my ears as I cupped them, barely muffling the sound. I was beginning to worry I would be imprisoned forever when the door swung open, getting my full attention. I looked up to see Aidan.

I blinked, wondering if I was hallucinating, then started to stand. Within seconds he had scooped me up in his arms and we were outside in the dim-lit basement hallway. The mother nurse who had whipped me was knocked out on the floor against the painted brick wall. Aidan rushed us past her as I closed my eyes, holding onto him as tightly as possible. Being with him again meant everything.

He took us to the end of the hallway to a big metal door. I was gently set down as he scrambled for the set of keys he'd stolen. I watched him try several before finding the right one, then he opened the heavy door revealing a brick tunnel with the same never-ending row of lights. Aidan took my hand in his as we stepped inside, shutting out the sound of the sirens.

"Are you alright?" He cupped my face in his hands, looking deep into my eyes. "Did she hurt you?"

"I'm fine."

"I'm sorry I couldn't get to you sooner." He wrapped me tightly in his arms, completely unaware of the freshly administered wounds throbbing beneath my shirt. I winced from the pain. He immediately released me, looking me over with concern.

"What's wrong? Did she hit you?"

I nodded, watching his eyes darken with anger. He looked toward the door, as if contemplating whether or not to go back and avenge the punishment that had been unleashed on me.

"Aidan, it's alright now." I touched his cheek, bringing his face toward me again. "Are we in the tunnels?"

"Yes." His expression was serious as he looked deep into my eyes. "Ivory, we have to make a decision. I can try to get us out of here, but we might get sick."

"I'm not going back. We would never see each other again and I can't live with that."

"But I don't want you to get sick."

"I'd rather take the risk of dying with you than have to spend an eternity without you."

Aidan's smile let me know that I had completely melted his heart. He gently grabbed my hand. "Can you run?"

I nodded, unsure if I truly could.

We rushed down what seemed to be an endless passage to nowhere as Aidan held on tight to my hand. The tunnel was a never-ending rectangle made out of solid red bricks. I had never known the true feeling of claustrophobia until that very moment. My throat began to burn with each breath, while my legs tried desperately to keep up. The pain in my back increased with each rapid rise and fall of my lungs. Within only a few minutes we reached another tunnel on the left that seemed to go on forever. Aidan stopped at the tunnel, his face tense with concentration. I tried to catch my breath but he encouraged me along, not seeming to be the least bit winded. We eventually passed four more tunnels that all looked the same. Only one was short enough to clearly reveal a metal door leading to one of the other buildings. I did my best to keep up with Aidan who stopped at every crossing, always asking how I was doing and if I was alright. He was hard at work trying to figure out the intricate puzzle. We followed the main passage all the way to another metal door where it came to a dead end. I began to wonder if we were trapped until Aidan led us to a sixth and last tunnel along the main vein. We turned left and continued to scurry along but my body gave out on me. I stopped, gasping for air. Aidan ran a hand over my cheeks and forehead.

"I'm sorry." He said, his eyes strained with concern. "I'm pretty sure this is a way out."

"I just need a break." I managed.

He swooped me up in his arms and carried both of us farther and farther down. I took advantage of his chivalry, resting my head and closing my eyes. My breath eventually returned to normal but I was deeply fatigued, starting to think about water and food. A sudden realization that those things would no longer be available made me anxious. I tried not to get too worked up, remembering that I had all I really needed. He seemed to be doing just fine, despite my extra weight.

Endless light, after light, after light began to give me a headache. It seemed like Aidan had been going forever. I would have guessed nearly an hour had gone by when he suddenly slowed and ascended a small set of stairs, still holding me firmly in his arms. He stopped at the top, carefully set me to my wobbly feet, then walked toward a door that looked different than the big heavy doors we'd seen earlier. This one was arched, set in a big metal frame with a small circular handle in the center. The paint was chipped and worn with age and rust scarred all exposed metal.

Aidan hesitated, then grabbed the handle and turned it with force. The circle complained with a screeching squeal, then the sound of a heavy click echoed throughout the tunnel walls. Aidan looked to me one last time before pulling the door open. I was instantly blinded.

Sunlight poured in, illuminating everything it touched. When my eyes began to adjust, I looked to see an open door to the world I had forever been restricted from. The same world I had dreamt of as a kid, the world I saw every day through the dreary institution windows. It was finally mine. I walked to the opening, already loving the smell of the fresh air. Aidan took my hand and we stepped out into the unknown.

the outside

L ittle plants sprouted from the ground, tickling my bare knees. The sun in its full glory re-energized my entire being. When I took in a deep breath, a soft breeze tantalized my nose with scents that were diverse and complex, like nothing I'd encountered in the greenhouse. I looked out in every direction and saw nothing but miles of thick forest. Vast expanses of dense trees and plants spread out before us in a variety of greens, browns and yellows. It was an enormous garden that went on forever.

We stood in awe, speechless, taking in the unfamiliar scenery around us. I broke away from Aidan's hand and twirled in the sun, happily enjoying its warmth. I released my hair, which fell loose from its bun. The sharp pins that always poked at my head flew to the ground. I felt so alive and wanted to touch every living thing in my path. Even the dirt and rocks at my feet were amazing.

I made my way to the nearest tree and rested my palms against its wide, strong trunk. One look up into the branches and I was breathless. It soared toward the heavens as far as I could see and seemed to brush the bright blue sky. The branches and leaves created a beautiful canopy that glittered in the sun. I smiled at the sky, excited to continue exploring. I knew I would never get tired of this infinite new world. I looked at Aidan who was watching me with an amused grin.

"Isn't this amazing?" I asked, still hugging the tree. "It's all so beautiful. This is exactly what I've dreamt of my entire life—to be here, doing this."

"I know." His smile widened.

I walked back to him, immediately burying myself in his arms. "Being here with you is everything I've ever wanted." I looked up into his eyes, happier than I'd ever been. His smile suddenly faded.

"What's wrong?"

"I just want to be able to take care of you and protect you. I know nothing about the land or how to survive."

"It doesn't matter, you've already done more than enough. We'll figure it out together."

He nuzzled into me, then his hands went to my torn clothing. "What did that woman do to you?"

I swallowed hard, trying not to remember the details. "She whipped me, twice."

"Unclothed?"

"Yes."

He looked infuriated all over again. "Can I see your back?"

I turned and held my hair aside as he carefully peeled the

clothing down. A gentle stroke near the wounds awakened my body to his touch.

He zipped me back up, then I spun around and looked into his sad eyes.

"The skin's not broken, but it's badly bruised," he said.

"It's not bothering me very much," I lied, although I knew he could see right through me. The old metal door caught my eye from behind him, still wide open. "What is the purpose of this door?" I asked.

He turned to look at it with a small frown. "I don't know for sure. Maybe it was used to transport supplies?"

"How did you know it was here?"

"I didn't, I just assumed the extra tunnel led somewhere else. I wasn't sure exactly where." He paused. "We must be quite far from the institution. I can't see it at all."

I never cared to see its ugly walls again. The trees were so thick it was impossible to see much of anything anyway. A tight suffocating reality hit me hard. I tried to push it away, but it wouldn't let up.

"Do you think we're already infected?"

"Ivory, there's no way to tell."

"How long do you think we have?" I asked, looking into the grave expression on Aidan's face.

"I don't know."

I focused again on the beauty around us.

Aidan firmly shut the door, then we headed away from it, our hands in a tight embrace.

We walked along, enjoying every second of our uninhibited freedom. We even skipped! After chasing each other around, hopping over rocks and playing silly made-up games, we found a small cove beneath a giant boulder to sit and rest.

I nestled up to Aidan who held me in the crook of his arm, being careful not to harm my injuries.

"I still can't believe that we're out here," I said, fingering one of the buttons on his shirt. "It feels like a dream."

"It does. So many nights I dreamt of us being free together."

"You did?"

"Yes."

I smiled as I remembered how brave and strong he'd been when rescuing me from that terrible torture room. Aidan was amazing. My stomach lurched with the realization that he could have been injured too.

"Did you get whipped?"

"No, I fought the teacher off."

"But, how did you find me?"

"I activated the sirens, then ran to the east wing basement…that vile woman was running down the hall. I tried two doors before I found you."

I laughed. "*You* activated the sirens? I thought they set them off *because* of you."

He chuckled.

"But how did you know where the tunnels were?"

"When they first brought me here, after I met with Oliver, we traveled in them from his mansion to the main building. I tried to memorize how many there were and where we came in. And today it all looked familiar."

"You're so smart. I could never do anything like that."

"Yes, you could."

I snuggled closer to him, taking his free hand in mine. "Is your finger alright?"

"It's fine. I think it looked worse than it was." He held it up, the line where it had been cut barely visible. "They sealed it nicely."

"I was worried about you."

"I know," he said, smiling.

We sat in a comfortable silence and enjoyed our rest together in the wilderness. I was tired from the day's drama, coming down from all the highs and lows. Overall, I was feeling content, despite our unavoidable obstacle. Even if the plague somehow didn't get to us, I knew we would probably die of starvation or exhaustion. Still, I couldn't help but wonder what was out there—if anything—and if we could possibly get to it.

"What are we going to do? Where will we go?"

"I thought we could just keep walking the way we have been, away from the institution," Aidan said.

"Do you think there are any survivors?"

"Maybe...there have to be remnants of the old world somewhere. If we keep walking, we might run into something, eventually, that will tell us what we need to know."

"What if no one survived and we're the only ones out here? The only ones left?"

"Then I feel lucky to be with you."

There was an eerie sense of peace, just the two of us. And somehow I knew, without any logical reason, that everything was going to be alright.

Aidan and I walked at a comfortable pace until the sun began to lower into the horizon. We stopped to watch the sky turn from gold, to orange, to pink, then purple, astonished by the natural beauty. Before the light faded completely, Aidan did his best to clear a spot for us to sleep. We sat there amongst the dark shadows of trees, staring up into the night sky. The twinkling stars captivated us for what seemed to be hours while my stomach reminded me I hadn't had dinner. In an attempt to keep warm, I pulled the white button-down shirt Aidan had given me over my shoulders. The air was comfortable, yet cool enough to chill my scrawny body.

Aidan lay beside me on the ground, using his forearm as a pillow. His crisp white t-shirt stood out in the soft glow of the moonlight. My eyes scanned his strong, muscular body. Before I knew it, I was wrapped tightly in his arms, safe and comfortable in the silence of the night. I relished the moment, soaking in every bit of him and the amazing feel of our embrace. His soft breath and warm arms lulled me into a welcome slumber.

✧ ✧ ✧

I awoke to tickles on my cheek, then a gentle brush. Another tickle trailed up my arm and another brush wiped it away. I opened my eyes, realizing Aidan's arm had been my pillow, then turned to see him watching me with a smirk.

"What are you doing?" I grinned.

"Look." He held up his hand where a tiny bug scurried along in a hurry.

I gasped sitting up. "Bugs! They're still alive!"

"And they like you." He smiled, brushing another from my arm.

I looked down to see a whole bunch of them crawling around on the ground. With a smile I scooped one onto my finger to examine it. The tiny creature had what looked to be two separate parts making up the head and butt, with a small line in-between. Its antennae were almost too small to see.

"Oh, I read about these. What are they called again?"

"Mmm, beetles?" Aidan looked to me in question.

"No." I frowned, examining the fast little bug crawling up my arm. "Ants! They're called ants. They make tunnels and build little mounds of dirt."

"Yes, I remember now."

"They're so adorable."

Aidan smiled, still playing with his own ant. "I wonder if they're somehow immune to the plague?"

"Maybe it's just not around here."

"Or maybe it's weakened."

"If they're still alive then there've got to be more bugs and possibly even animals that made it," I said.

"I thought I saw a bird earlier, but I wasn't sure."

"Really? How long have you been awake?"

"A while."

I blushed. "You've been watching me sleep?"

"I couldn't resist. I've decided that waking up to you is the best thing I've ever done."

I looked into his sweet sincere eyes, still amazed by the effect he had on me. Nobody had ever made me feel so special, so loved and so incredibly beautiful.

"So, what are our plans for today?" I asked.

"Walking, walking and more walking. Are you thrilled?"

"Yes."

He chuckled. "Me too."

The sky was a beautiful shade of blue. A small breeze ruffled the limbs of the trees, causing the leaves to dance and shimmer in the sun's warm rays. Aidan and I walked amongst the beauty, still enthralled by everything in sight. We often stopped to examine a tree or bush and took the time to play and be silly. Everything felt so right, just the two of us. The only uncomfortable element was having to pee and my stomach pains that seemed to get worse by the hour. I tried to ignore the latter as much as I could, never complaining, though it was hard. Our entire lives we'd lived by a very strict schedule and didn't even have the slightest clue what hunger was. I had quickly figured out that it wasn't pleasant at all.

As we stopped beside a small creek, I began to wonder what fresh water would taste like.

"Do you think this water would be alright to drink?" I asked, my throat getting drier by the minute.

"I don't think we should risk it, just in case." A hint of worry traced Aidan's eyes. "Are you really thirsty?"

"A little."

"Maybe we'll run into something—like an old store, or anything that might help us out, you know?"

I nodded, still wanting to drink the water. "So, it probably wouldn't be a good idea to eat anything either?"

"I don't think we should, Ivory. Are you really hungry?"

"Aren't you?"

"I've been ignoring it."

"Me too, but it keeps coming back."

"If we don't find a store by this time tomorrow, we'll eat the safest plants and water we can find."

"That sounds reasonable."

By the time the sky was beginning to put on its magnificent show of colors, I was not feeling so well. I didn't want to complain, but my stomach was not just hungry—it was starving. My body reacted with deep hunger pains and an enormous headache that I couldn't shake. On top of that I was starting to lose my balance; I felt lightheaded and woozy.

Aidan suggested we stop for the day and rest, and led me to a patch of soft greenery. He stroked his hand over my face and hair, seeming more anxious about me by the minute. I could tell he was just as run down and miserable as I was, though he never said a word about it.

"We probably should have eaten something," he said. "I'll go see what I can find."

"No! Don't leave me. It's getting too dark anyway."

He took a second to answer, his hand leaving my face. "I don't know what to do, Ivory. I feel so helpless."

"It's alright."

"No, it's not."

"Yes, it is," I argued, giving him a smile. "I just want you to hold me. That always makes me feel better."

He lay facing me, and looked into my eyes as he held me close. "I'm sorry this is so miserable."

"It'll get better tomorrow. We'll find something to eat."

Aidan continued to stroke my tangled hair, the repetitive motion comforting me into a drowsy state. I focused as hard as I could on the sensation of his loving touch, ignoring my stomach until sleep took me away. Yet even sleep was not peaceful; I tossed and turned all night long.

I awoke alone in a state of panic. Aidan was gone! My restless night had made my headache and stomachache one hundred times worse. I sat up, getting a terrible head rush as I looked around in every direction. The sun was just peeking up through the trunks of the trees, its bronze light momentarily blinding me.

A sudden rustle through the woods got my attention. I turned to see Aidan walking toward me holding up the bottom of his shirt. He looked to have a lot more energy than he'd had the night before.

"Good morning." He knelt before me. "I've got breakfast!"

"You do?" I braced myself; ready to see twigs and leaves.

He opened his shirt to reveal a huge pile of blackberries and raspberries, which just happened to be my favorite fruit. I practically fainted on the spot before wolfing down as many as I possibly could. Surprisingly, it didn't take long to get full from the tart little berries. My body instantly reacted to the rush of sugar, which gave me an immediate boost of energy. Within minutes it was obvious that we were both feeling a whole lot better. I thanked him a million times then we played, tossing the fruit back and forth into each other's mouths. We giggled the morning away, eventually continuing our never-ending walk.

I didn't understand why, especially since we'd had a nice breakfast, but a little after noon I started to feel terrible again. The headache and stomach pains came back so severely I could hardly walk. My muscles had begun to ache as well, making me feel truly ill. That's when I started to wonder if I had gotten the plague.

While we rested seated on a fallen tree, I began to cry.

"Ivory?" Aidan's worried-sick expression only made me cry harder.

"I just feel so terrible," I sobbed. "I thought I was doing better and that everything was going to be fine and now I just... I just can't take it anymore."

"What do you want to do? What do you want me to do? Should I go find some more berries?"

I shook my head. "No."

Aidan looked like he was about to crack. He wiped my tears away.

"I think I might be sick," I admitted, hating the way the words sounded out loud.

His face lost some color. "You do?"

"I don't know. I don't know what else it could be, besides not drinking any water."

"Well, let's go find some." He stood, looking in every direction.

"I can't walk anymore, at least not right now."

"Then I'll carry you." Before I could protest he had me in his arms, walking over challenging terrain.

"I don't want to drain all of your energy, too," I said, burying my face in his neck.

"I'm fine."

I closed my eyes, relaxing my weary body in Aidan's strong arms. Delirious and drained, I wasn't sure how much time had gone by when he finally stopped.

"Do you hear that?" he asked.

I listened to hear a loud roaring sound off in the distance. "What is it?"

"I would guess it's a big river."

"Water?" I asked, my mind still not completely in the present.

"Yes."

It seemed like he had only taken a few steps, when the sound got louder and louder.

"There it is!" he exclaimed.

I looked a little ways ahead of us to see a large stream of water flowing rapidly through the trees. I knew in an instant that it was exactly what I needed. I turned to Aidan with the best smile I could muster up, noticing he was fatigued.

"You can set me down now," I said.

"Are you sure?"

I nodded, trying to regain my balance as he put me down. I held on tightly to him, looking deep into his eyes.

"Are you alright?" I asked, worried about his condition.

"I'm looking forward to that water."

"Me too, come on." I was just about to lead us to the river when something behind me distracted his eyes. His expression went from tired to shocked within seconds.

"What is it?" I looked toward the water to see two people walking along the bank: a man and a woman who appeared to be a few years older than Aidan. The man wore a dark t-shirt and torn light blue pants, his hair short and disheveled. The woman had shoulder length light brown hair and wore a flowing skirt and revealing shoulder-less top. They each carried a long painted stick with loops and the man was also carrying a large bucket. My eyes flew open.

"Survivors!" I yelled.

"You see it too?"

"Yes," I chuckled, getting a smirk out of him.

"I thought I was hallucinating."

"Maybe they can help us."

We started toward them.

"Wait," Aidan stopped me. "What if they're dangerous?"

"Dangerous? How?"

"We're not supposed to be out here. What if they send us back to the institution?"

I frowned, thinking about it for a moment. "They're probably just happy to be alive. I'm sure if we explain the situation, they'll understand."

Aidan still looked skeptical.

"Aidan, we don't have much of a choice, do we?"

He nodded, as we headed toward the first surviving human beings we'd ever seen since our escape.

refuge

The man noticed us first, his face in a complete state of shock. He stopped abruptly, giving the woman a hint that something was up. She had the same wide-eyed, jaw-dropped expression at first; then her mouth softened and she gave a big smile.

"Oh, Rowen. Children!" she exclaimed, walking toward us very carefully. "Hello."

"Hello." Aidan's voice was anxious.

We stopped a few feet away, careful not to get too close. Our worn shoes sunk into the muddy pebbles on the bank.

"Are you okay?" the woman said with what seemed to be genuine concern.

What must we have looked like to them, unkempt and dirty from our days in the wild?

"We need help," Aidan answered. "My friend is sick."

She frowned. "Sick with what?"

"It must be the plague," Aidan said.

The couple exchanged a knowing glance, then the man called Rowen looked to us with sympathetic eyes.

"Why don't you come with us? We've got a small community just over the hill with plenty of food and water. We can get you care there."

"Alright," I nodded, a tremendous feeling of relief washing over me.

"I'm Hydra," the woman said, placing a hand on her chest. "This is Rowen."

"My name is Ivory."

"And I am Aidan."

They both smiled, seeming pleased.

Aidan and I followed them on a well-worn path through the woods, both of us tense and uncomfortable. The couple seemed to be just as nervous as we were, unsure of what to say or how to act. I took it as a good sign.

"How long have you been out here?" Rowen asked, still trudging along.

"Two and a half days," Aidan answered.

"Without food or water?"

"Yes."

"And you came from the institution?" Hydra asked, causing Aidan to stop. She immediately responded to his reaction. "It's okay, you're safe with us."

The rest of the walk was quiet as I stayed close to Aidan's side. We finally broke out of the woods and into a clearing that looked to be a camp of sorts. Multiple little cabins were spread out on either side of a small creek. One big house sat in the middle, right along the creek's edge.

"This is our home." Rowen said, looking proud.

As my eyes took in the neat little community, I saw people going from building to building, some in groups, some standing alone doing tasks. One girl who looked about my age stood in front of a long rope strung between two cabins attaching clothes to it.

"There are others?" I asked.

"Yes," Hydra said, smiling. "Many others."

Aidan and I exchanged glances before we followed Rowen and Hydra to the camp. Every person outside seemed to stop what they were doing and stare intently at us. More and more people emerged from the cabins just to get a look. I was amazed by the variety in age, seeing some looking grey and even a few small children. I began to wonder how all of them survived the plague and what they were doing living here.

We stopped in front of the house. Hydra gave her stick to a woman and asked another to get us some water.

"Ivory, do you want to come with me to the physician?" she asked.

I nodded, looking to Aidan. The thought of being away from him made me anxious.

"Come with me?" I asked, already knowing he wouldn't want me to go alone.

"Of course."

After drinking tons of the best water I'd ever tasted, they guided us to one of the bigger cabins that was set up like a clinic. The walls were painted a cheery light peach with a few pictures of art on the wall—which I didn't understand, but liked. Hydra led me to a small room where a cot lay before me, along with a long counter with various medical supplies and tools. My insides squirmed.

"If you want to go ahead and lie down, Deidra, our nurse should be here any minute."

Nurse. The word in combination with the cot made me feel faint. I hesitated, looking to Aidan who was standing beside me.

"I'll leave you alone for a few minutes, to get settled," Hydra said. She seemed uncomfortable.

I looked into Aidan's weary eyes, having flashes of the terrible experience I'd had in the basement of the institution. The thought of having to have the same examination repeated with Aidan in the room was unbearable. My cheeks heated instantly.

"If she makes me get undressed—"

"I'll leave the room." He traced my face with his eyes. "What's wrong?"

"In the institution..." It was hard to get out. "She did something else to me."

He frowned. "What?"

"Ah, there you are." A plump middle-aged woman with short greying hair and a big friendly smile walked in. "I'm Deidra, the nurse and midwife."

"Midwife?" I questioned.

"For babies," she said, with a grin. "You must be Ivory."

"Yes."

Aidan quickly introduced himself, then she had me sit on the cot while he sat in a chair. I was suddenly nauseous.

"So, what are your symptoms, dear?" She peered at me from underneath small glasses.

"Headache, stomachache—my muscles hurt."

"But you've been out in the wild for nearly three days?"

"Yes."

"Okay."

She checked my pulse and blood pressure, which was nothing new; it had been a standard procedure in the institution. Then she took me to a scale, measured my height and weight and had me sit back on the cot.

"I'm just going to ask you a few questions." She looked to me, then Aidan, a pad of paper and pen gripped firmly in her hands. "Is that okay?"

I nodded.

"When was your last menstrual period?"

Aidan's eyebrow arched, nearly making me laugh. I was glad he had no idea what she was talking about; the boys were not taught about feminine health issues in the institution.

"I don't know."

"Have you ever had one?"

"Yes."

Deidra peered at me, as if trying to find something. "Have you had sex recently?"

"Sex?" I questioned, having no idea what she was talking about. "What is that?"

"Oh, dear," she chuckled. "Intercourse? Coitus?"

I frowned and shook my head, even more confused.

"Mating?"

Realizing at last what she meant, I was instantly embarrassed and blushed. Aidan wasn't a help, giggling in his chair.

"No!"

"Okay," she said as she stood. "Well, other than being dehydrated, exhausted, famished and needing to gain some weight, I'd say you're in perfect health."

"Really? It's not the plague?"

She studied my face. "No, dear. The plague has been nonexistent for years."

I took a minute to soak in her words, not able to believe it.

"What?" Aidan asked, looking just as taken aback as I was. "What do you mean?"

"Everyone developed a natural immunity to it over twenty years ago."

"That's impossible," Aidan stated. "I watched an entire institution die from it two years ago."

Deidra stared at Aidan for a few seconds, then averted her eyes. "They must have kept it completely contained and confidential because we didn't hear of it. Why don't you mention it to Rowen? He knows more about those things than I do."

"It *is* still a threat," Aidan warned. "We should take the proper precautions." He looked at me with concern.

"Well, even if it were still a threat, Ivory here is just fine. The plague's symptoms were very obvious and recognizable."

Aidan's look of frustration didn't fade as Deidra led us out of the cabin and into the big modern log home. Inside it was spacious and light with many large windows, a huge fireplace and multiple bedrooms and bathrooms. I couldn't help but feel comfortable in the cozy, clean-smelling home that was neatly decorated unlike anything I'd ever seen. Different colors of paint, art of all different kinds and photographs strategically covered the walls, creating a very personal atmosphere.

My eyes flickered over the interior, trying to take in everything. We followed Deidra to a large, beautiful kitchen where Rowen, Hydra and a couple others were preparing food. My nose was tantalized with smells of herbs and spices. I admired the shiny black countertops, silver appliances and artfully crafted golden cupboards.

"Ivory, Aidan..." Rowen smiled seeing us, "come sit in the dining room, your meals are almost done."

My stomach grumbled. "You made us food?"

He laughed. "Of course. You must be starving."

The dining room was impressive, with a large wooden table and at least twelve chairs filling the long room. A huge view of the cabins and expansive forest was visible through two big windows.

I sat in a chair next to Aidan's, still admiring everything around me. Rowen set two glasses of water before us, then sat at the head of the table.

"What do you think?" He asked. "Is this all just a little overwhelming?"

"Deidra mentioned that the plague has been extinct for some time now, but that cannot be..." Aidan told Rowen about the institution that was once his home and what he had seen.

Rowen's expression turned very serious. "You say this was two years ago?"

"Yes."

"And that is why they moved you?"

Aidan nodded, a stern frown upon his face.

Rowen was silent for a minute, his mind hard at work. "I'm not sure, but what you remember seeing and what actually happened could be two completely different things."

"Meaning what?"

"They have very effective methods of brainwashing children."

"Brainwash? No, what I saw was real!" Aidan seemed to be getting more and more upset. "Why would they brainwash me? There would be no reason to."

Rowen seemed to choose his words carefully. "Aidan, the institutions are dying. There are only five left. They want others to believe it is still a threat, which is why they would do such a thing. Your institution was probably one that had fallen."

"So what you're saying is that I've been brainwashed and all of my memories are false?"

"Like I said, there is no way to know for sure. I do know for a fact that the plague is no longer in existence, so there has to be some other explanation for what you experienced."

Aidan shook his head in disbelief.

"I know it's a lot for you to handle right now—"

"How are you so sure that what I experienced was false? The institutions are dying because the plague is supposedly gone?" Aidan asked.

"Yes."

"So, basically what you're telling me is that we've both been lied to and made to think we were in danger our entire lives, when truthfully we were never in any kind of danger at all?"

"It seems so, yes."

"That's very hard to believe."

"I can imagine it is."

"And it doesn't make any sense. Why would they do that? For what purpose?"

"It's all very complicated."

"Why should I trust you?"

"Aidan..." I said, after all these people were being so nice to us.

"I'm not asking you to, but I do think you should keep an open mind. There is still a lot to explain. The state of the world is very different than what you might think."

"Is it?"

"Yes," Rowen answered.

"Then enlighten me," Aidan said, sitting back, ready to listen.

"I think the information I have given you is more than

enough for today, Aidan, especially this day when you are both so tired and worn down."

Aidan opened his mouth to talk, but Rowen didn't give him a chance.

"You are more than welcome to stay here. We have a spare bedroom in the basement and a second one, if you wish. There are plenty of extra clothes and supplies to go around."

"Thank you," I said, grateful for his kindness.

A pretty girl with dark brown hair walked in from the kitchen with two steaming hot plates. She set one each in front of Aidan and me, and a large meal of chicken, bread, corn and sliced apples also sat before us. I had never been so happy to see food in my entire life. After another thank you, I dug in and tried my best not to embarrass myself. The food worked like magic in my body, each bite slowly bringing me back to life.

Hydra walked to Rowen, placed her hands on his shoulders for a moment, then joined us at the table. I couldn't help but wonder if they were related or something else. It was the something else that piqued my interest.

"Are you brother and sister?" I asked, between a bite of corn and chicken.

Hydra smiled. "No. We're together—partners."

I nodded, not completely understanding.

"Are you...?" Her words trailed off as she looked to Aidan and me.

"We're not related," I said.

"Just friends?"

"More than friends," Aidan said, making me smile.

"So you are together?"

"Yes."

Hydra smiled. "I thought so… Don't feel ashamed or like

you're doing something wrong. It's a beautiful thing for you to be together. We want you to feel comfortable here; it's nothing like the institutions. You're free to be who you are or who you want to be."

"What is this place?" Aidan asked.

"We are a self-sustained, peaceful community. We're all very hardworking and respectful of ourselves and each other."

"And everyone has a task or chore?"

"In a way, yes. But we're all doing things that we love best. Nobody is forced to do anything."

"Who is the leader?"

"There is no leader. We are all equal."

"Surely, there has to be order of some kind?"

Rowen laughed. "There's lots of 'order,' just no one yelling demands."

"I don't understand," Aidan said, frowning.

"You will," Rowen smiled. "I will explain everything, I promise."

❖ ❖ ❖

It was very evident that both Aidan and I were feeling tremendously better by the time our plates were empty. Our moods were lifted and there was a sudden joyful spirit in the air.

Rowen and Hydra took us for a quick tour throughout the upper part of the house, which still left me breathless. The vaulted ceilings, windows that looked out through the roof and big loft were unlike anything I'd ever seen. We followed Rowen and Hydra across the shiny wood floors to a staircase that took us down to the spacious basement. Two huge windows looked out to the wild and a long, padded bench filled the entire space. We were led to one of five doors within a hallway and taken into a small cozy bedroom. A large, beautifully adorned bed sat amongst matching furniture, stirring up thoughts that were beyond my control. The concept of sharing a bed with Aidan overwhelmed my body with tingles.

"This is our spare bedroom. You're welcome to sleep here or wherever you'd be more comfortable."

Aidan looked inquisitive, questioning me with his eyes.

"Thank you," I said. "This will work wonderfully."

"For both of you?" Rowen and Aidan stared at me for an answer, curiosity written all over them.

"Yes."

"Ivory," Hydra turned to me, "if you want to come upstairs I can get you some clothes and other necessities?"

"Alright."

I glanced at Aidan, getting a content smile in return.

The fears and anxieties I had experienced earlier were completely gone, allowing me to relax and trust Hydra to take care of me. She led me to a large bedroom that was decorated with paraphernalia from cultures of all different kinds and periods. A big bed with wooden posts sat in the middle with shiny, fancy bedding. Hydra opened a small room with nothing but clothes, shoes and accessories. She walked in and rifled through row after row of neatly piled clothing.

"Okay, so..." she turned to eye me, "about what size are you? Do you know?"

I looked down at my torn institution uniform covered with dirt. "No."

"You're really petite, so, I think..." She paused to pull out a pair of blue pants the same material as Rowen's. "Here, these should fit."

She handed me the pants as I gently unfolded them, inspecting the uniquely embroidered pockets and overall design.

"Do you prefer skirts or pants?" she asked, pulling clothes out into a stack on the floor.

"Pants, definitely pants."

"You should try those jeans on so we know what size you are, then we can go from there."

"These are called jeans?"

She smiled. "Yes."

"Oh."

"You can use our bathroom." She pointed to another room within the room.

I walked to the dark space, unsure of how to light it.

"Hydra? How do I turn the light on?"

She grinned and walked to where I stood in the doorway. With a "click" the lights were on.

"Thank you." I practiced flicking the lights off and on for a couple of seconds before walking in and closing the door behind me. As I began to pull my clothes off, the first thing my eyes went to was a bright red fuzzy carpet and big red towels hanging nearby. Then I was distracted by the biggest bathtub I'd ever seen with strange vents lining the middle. A huge glass encased shower made of rock stood in the corner, looking extremely inviting. The thought of clean water running over my body gave me goose bumps.

I pulled the pants on over my undershorts, buttoning them without any effort at all. The fabric slouched from my waist, threatening to fall. I was just about to walk to one of two sinks when a movement scared me half to death. I looked up to see a girl appearing startled, her long light blonde hair tousled around her small face. She was dirty, and purple shadows darkened the skin beneath her tired eyes. Somehow, regardless of it all, she was beautiful.

It was me.

It took me a couple of seconds to fully register that I was in fact looking at myself. I had to move a body part or two just to confirm it. The bathroom became a stage as I moved all around to see what I looked like with different expressions and at different angles. I scanned every inch of me, looking at my face in its entirety and checking out my diminutive figure. My eyes were in fact the same color of the sky, just as Flora had always said, and my wavy blonde locks bounced with every movement. My skin somehow didn't look too bad seeing it all at the same time. I decided that, all in all, I was quite pretty.

"Ivory? Are you okay in there?" Hydra's muffled voice startled me.

"Yes."

"Do they fit?"

I walked out wearing the pants and my dirty white blouse. "No."

"Too big?"

I nodded.

She tossed me another pair. "Here, try these, they're a little smaller."

"Alright." I headed back to the bathroom.

"Wait, here are some shirts for you to try too. And if you'd like, you're welcome to take a shower."

"I'd like that very much!"

The second pair of pants ended up fitting just right and I had fun trying on all of the different styles and shapes of shirts. My favorite and most flattering was a plain black t-shirt that clung to my skin, showing off my tiny waist. The fabric was unbelievably soft and comfortable. I ended up with three pairs of pants, five shirts, a package of socks, six pairs of underwear of an unfamiliar style, two lacy bras, a couple hooded jackets, black lace-up boots and a whole kit of toiletries and girl necessities. Hydra assured me that it was all just to get me started and that she would be on the lookout for more clothes. It was more than I knew what to do with. I couldn't have been more grateful.

When we were finally finished with my outfitting, the only thing on my mind was getting clean. I grabbed a set of clothes, then locked myself in the bathroom, enjoying showering in hot water for the first time in my life. I took my time cleaning and shampooing, allowing the water to fully relax every single muscle. I stepped out of the shower feeling euphoric, rejuvenated and ready for sleep. After slipping on my tight black t-shirt, bright red underwear and flattering pants called jeans, I went back out to the bedroom to find Hydra lying on her bed with a book. Her eyes lit up at the sight of me.

"Wow," she chuckled. "You look like a completely different person."

"I feel like a different person. Thank you."

"Aidan's going to be stunned."

"Where is he?"

"Getting the same treatment you are."

I smiled to myself, wondering what he would look like in clothes like Rowen's.

"How long have you two been together?" She asked, setting her book aside.

"Not long. We never really had a chance to be together in the institution."

"I bet."

"How long have you and Rowen been together?"

"Five years."

"That's a long time... Do you sleep in the same bed with him?"

She laughed. "Yes, all of the couples do. It's a normal thing."

"So, it's alright for Aidan and I to sleep in the same bed?"

"Of course it is, if it's what you want."

"What about holding hands around others?"

"Showing affection is healthy and necessary—especially if you love someone." She paused. "Do you love Aidan?"

"Yes, I love him very much."

A grin lightened her face. "You don't have to hide anything anymore, Ivory. You'll see what things are like here and you'll get used to it. We are very affectionate and loving people."

I gathered some of my things as Hydra hopped from the bed and grabbed a handful herself. We went downstairs to the spare room where she helped me put everything away in the large wooden dresser opposite the bed. I had just set the last pair of socks in their place when a movement from the doorway caught my eye. I turned to see Aidan looking clean, polished and absolutely gorgeous.

A dark grey t-shirt sculpted his upper body, showing off his broad, toned shoulders. Loose black pants with big side pockets added to the appeal, making him appear even more masculine. His hair was still damp, naturally shaped into tiny spikes and his eyes looked a shade darker, complimented by the steel color of his shirt. I was suddenly shy and intimidated by the beautiful boy in front of me -- until he smiled.

Hydra mumbled a few words about making ourselves at home before leaving us alone in our room together. Aidan set his pile of clothes aside then walked to me, his face struck with fascination.

"You look incredible," he said, still taking me all in. I was sure to note that his eyes never once left me from the moment he stepped in the door. "Not that you didn't before, because I thought you were adorable covered in dirt."

I laughed and took a good look at his new clothes up close, thinking they looked even better. "We're all shiny and new."

With a smile he tugged at the hem of my shirt, thumbing the soft fabric. His hands went to either side of my hips as he admired the jeans. I fell into him, getting a big loving hug. He grabbed a handful of my hair and inhaled.

"You smell so good." He nuzzled into me. "How do you feel?"

"I'm feeling much better, besides being really tired."

"Me too."

I looked up into his eyes, feeling a flush coming on. "Will you lie with me? Then we can go to sleep?"

He smiled. "Yes."

Aidan and I got ourselves ready for bed in the basement bathroom, each of us taking turns changing and preparing for a long night's sleep. I stood in our room, wearing a comfortable pair of drawstring pants and my black t-shirt, and waited for Aidan to finish. Unsure of what to do, I practiced putting my hair up with a small band, then organized and sorted through my clothes. Aidan walked in wearing his t-shirt and pajama pants similar to mine. We smiled at each other, then I watched as he turned down the covers and sat on one edge.

He looked at me with curious eyes. "Are you alright with this? Because I don't want to make you uncomfortable."

I shut my drawer and walked to the bed, sitting beside him. "It's just that we've been taught our whole lives that this is wrong, so it feels a little strange. I don't know what to do with myself."

"Do you want me to sleep somewhere else?"

"No, I love sleeping with you. I just have to get used to this setting, you know?"

He nodded.

I crawled onto the bed and settled myself underneath the covers. Aidan turned to me, getting himself situated. We automatically tangled ourselves into each other as if still on the freezing earth floor.

"I can't believe we made it," I said. "Without dying of the plague or starving to death. I really thought we were going to die out there."

"I did too. I'm glad you're well, and I'm glad we still have time together."

I focused on Aidan's hand as he rubbed the small of my back.

"Wasn't that the best meal you've ever had in your entire life?" he asked.

"Yes, actually, it was."

"Amazing how good food tastes when you haven't had it for so long."

"What do you think of this place?"

"I'm not sure. They are all very nice but I'm still confused about what Rowen said. What I saw was real, I don't care what he says."

"Aidan, how could there only be five institutions left? And if the plague is truly gone, then why would we still be forced to live our lives in the institution? It makes no sense."

"No, it doesn't, which is why I'm going to find out exactly what's going on tomorrow."

"Do you think we'll stay here?"

"I don't know."

We rested in silence for a while, both of us still perplexed by the whole situation. Our tired brains could barely handle the current reality, let alone a completely different concept.

I took in a deep breath and listened to creaks and cracks of footsteps from above.

"What is a menstrual period?"

Aidan's question made me burst into laughter.

"You don't miss a thing, do you?" I smiled, looking at his playful expression. "It's just something that happens to females."

"Only females?"

"Yes."

"What is it?"

"You don't want to know."

"But I do."

I laughed. "No, you don't. Do inexplicable things happen to your body that you can't control?"

His eyes got huge. "Yes! All the time."

"Really?" I frowned, a little alarmed. "Like what?"

He looked down, his face flushing. "It's a little difficult to explain."

I smiled. "Should I be worried?"

"No, I think it's normal."

"Alright."

I nestled into him, loving the smell of soap and fresh linen.

"What did you mean earlier when you said the mother nurse did something else to you?"

I cringed. "It's nothing. It doesn't matter anymore."

"You seemed upset. Was it something terrible?"

"Yes, but I'm fine."

"Are you sure?"

I nodded into him, not wanting to think about it anymore. My mind scrambled for another subject. "Did Rowen ask you about us?"

"No."

"Hydra says it's alright for us to touch in front of people. She says it's normal."

"Really? It's going to take me a while to get used to that."

"Me too." I closed my eyes, suddenly aware of just how tired I was.

"Who's going to turn the lights off?"

I looked to see Aidan squinting into the light on the ceiling. His expression made me giggle. "I suspect you are."

He gave me a smirk. "I was expecting it to turn off automatically." I laughed as he jumped off the bed, flipped the switch, then got back underneath the covers with me. "I have to get used to this light thing, too."

Within seconds our eyes adjusted to the dim light coming through the dark window fabric. I could feel my body shutting down. I looked into Aidan's sweet sleepy eyes one last time before closing my own. He held me snug in his arms as my entire being melted into his warmth.

"I love you, Ivory."

awakening

I awoke warm and comfortable swaddled in blankets and Aidan's loving hold. I questioned where I was until images of the eventful day before slowly crept back into my thoughts—along with an uncontrollable urge to pee. I leapt from the bed and into the small bathroom, noticing just how sleepy my reflection looked before emptying my bladder. After splashing my face and combing fingers through my hair, I went back to Aidan who was still sound asleep underneath the covers. I slowly crawled back onto the bed beside him, propping my head up on an elbow to watch his peaceful slumber. My eyes scanned every inch of his face, admiring how tranquil and content he was. I watched the rise and fall movement of his chest, listened to his soft breath and smiled when he stirred, eventually opening his tired eyes. He looked to me, then around the room as if wondering about his surroundings as I had.

"Good morning," I chimed.

"Good morning," he said smiling. "Have you been awake long?"

"No, just long enough to watch you for a while." I squirmed under the blankets and pressed against his warm body.

"I wonder what time it is?"

"I don't know, but it looks bright out." I peered at the covered window. "I suppose we should go find other living beings."

"Or we could stay here forever locked away in this room."

"I like that idea, but I'm hungry."

He smiled. "Then we better go get you the best breakfast ever."

We got ourselves together and dressed then headed upstairs. The house was bright and alive with noise, though I didn't see anyone until we stepped into the living room. Rowen and Hydra sat on one of two wide chairs, cuddled up to each other with a book in each of their hands. I noticed Rowen's arm wrapped around Hydra, who had a hand resting on his thigh.

Rowen spotted us immediately. He closed his book and tossed it to the floor.

"Hey, you two," he grinned. "I was beginning to wonder if you were ever going to join us."

Hydra smiled up at us. "Did you have a good rest?"

"Yes, thank you," I said.

"I'm guessing you're probably hungry," Rowen said, standing from his seat.

"Yes, shall we make our own food?" Aidan asked.

"No, I'll whip you up some eggs and toast. Just relax."

I wasn't sure I knew how to relax.

"Come, sit." Hydra motioned toward the other chair and Aidan and I sat beside each other. A girl with a basket of clothes walked across the room, then disappeared into the hall.

"So, what are your tasks?" Aidan asked.

"Well, mostly I tend to this house. Keep up on housework, cleaning and making sure everyone has what they need. Occasionally, I cook and maintain the food and every once in a while I learn care-taking skills from Deidra."

"How long have you been here?"

"As long as I can remember."

"You were born here?"

"No, my parents kept me hidden and out of the institutions, they didn't want me to be taken away from them. When they got sick they sent me to live with my uncle who brought me here. It was all very primitive and only a few families lived here at the time, but it soon became my home and has been ever since."

"And Rowen?"

"He was rescued nine years ago."

"From an institution?"

"Yes. He knows exactly how you feel."

That fact was comforting.

"What does he do?"

"Rowen is a jack-of-all-trades. He loves doing everything, especially maintenance work."

"Are there schedules and times at which certain things must be done?"

"Yes."

"Where is that written?"

Hydra smiled. "It's all memorized. Everyone knows what they need to do when they need to do it. We all work together and keep things running smoothly.

"After breakfast we would love to show you around and give you an idea of exactly what goes on and where everything is. You can meet everyone and find out what it's like here."

"That would be wonderful," I said, excited for the day.

"Is there a time when Rowen might answer some questions?" Aidan asked.

"You can try him at breakfast, but yes, he would love to answer all of your questions and talk to you about everything. I know you're curious and there is much to tell."

There was a moment of silence until Rowen walked in the room with a spatula. "It's almost done."

"Okay." Hydra smiled at him and watched him disappear back into the kitchen. She turned to look at us, her face suddenly apprehensive. "Mind if I ask you a few questions?"

"Go ahead," Aidan permitted, his expression contemplative.

"How did you get out of the institution?"

"We escaped through the underground tunnels."

"Did you plan it?"

"No. It happened by chance."

"Did you want to escape?"

"Yes."

"Why?"

"Things got complicated and…we just wanted to be together."

"I understand," Hydra said with compassion.

There was a moment of silence before we shuffled to the dining room where plates of food for all of us sat, along with napkins, silverware and drinks. My stomach grumbled as we took our places to eat. Aidan and I thanked Rowen again before digging in.

"I'm looking forward to showing you our community," Rowen said. "I think you will enjoy it."

"What is the state of the world now that the plague is gone?" Aidan asked, setting down his fork. "Surely it must be peaceful?"

Rowen chuckled. "You don't beat around the bush at all do you?"

"Beat a bush?" Aidan frowned. "I don't know what you mean."

"Nevermind." Rowen's smile faded. "There are other issues now."

Aidan stared at him for more.

"The world is in a state of chaos. There's been a war going on for years."

"What kind of war?" Aidan asked.

Rowen sighed, setting down his fork to use his napkin. He took a drink of water, then looked back to Aidan. "Why don't we save the heavy conversation for later? We should enjoy the day."

"If you insist."

After finishing breakfast, Hydra quickly gathered the dishes and handed them off to a girl called Rayne, then we all went outside in the bright midday sunshine. I couldn't get over how incredible it felt to be able to step outside whenever I pleased. It was a freedom I thoroughly enjoyed after being cooped up my entire life.

Rowen led us on a small dirt path beside the creek where I listened to the water gurgle below. I couldn't help but notice a few curious faces staring our way.

"There are about forty-five of us here now. Some of us

travel to different regions for trading and other purposes. We've also got a handful of men at war."

"Do they come back?" I asked.

"Some do, yes. At least one will come back to give us news. Right now things are looking good, but we'll discuss all of that later."

Rowen pointed to the row of cabins to the side and front of us. "Each cabin has running water and electricity, which we are very proud of. Not all communities have the luxury."

"Really?" Aidan asked.

"We're lucky enough to have a small town nearby that converted everything to wind and solar energy long before the plague hit. A couple of our men were mechanically inclined enough to figure out how to maintain the wind turbines."

"Who takes care of the water?"

"There's an underground well, so it's pretty self-sufficient. Ground water is pumped into the cabins. We do test the water regularly, just to make sure everything is clean and useable."

"How is it that the institutions have running water and electricity?" Aidan asked. "Do they use the same methods?"

"No. Well, some might, but the institutions are funded and workers are paid to take care of all of that." He paused. "Anyway, each unit has its own washing machine, kitchen, bedrooms and at least one bathroom. Everyone within each cabin prepares their own meals and cares for themselves."

"How many are in each cabin?"

"Up to four."

"And are they all related?"

"Not by blood, no. Some are, but very few. We consider ourselves to be family in a friendly way, understand?"

Aidan nodded. "Is there a rhyme or reason to where people live?"

"Not really. They live where they want to. Mostly there are friends living with friends, some relatives live together and couples live together."

A boy that appeared to be Aidan's age with rippling muscles under a sleeveless black shirt smiled as we approached him. He seemed to be repairing the outside of a cabin.

"Hey, Talon," Rowen greeted him. "This is Ivory and Aidan. They are new to our community."

"Hi." Talon hooked his hammer into a tan belt around his waist then held his hand out to Aidan. "Nice to meet you."

"Nice to meet you, too, Talon."

They briefly shook hands, then Talon's eyes went to me. He gave me a friendly nod. "Hi."

"Hello."

"Talon is one of our carpenters," Rowen said. "He can build just about anything."

"That's interesting," Aidan remarked.

"I could show you what I know," Talon offered, seeming eager to be a teacher.

"I'd like that—very much."

"We'll see you later, Talon. Keep up the good work." Rowen and Talon exchanged a handshake before we continued down the path.

"He seems nice," Aidan commented.

"Yes, and he's a hard worker. The only thing about Talon is he's the wolf of the pack."

"Rowen..." Hydra warned.

"What do you mean?" Aidan asked.

"He's a womanizer, which means you should probably watch your girl around him, know what I mean?"

"Ivory?"

"Oh, yeah. Unless you make it clear that she's yours, he'll be all over her."

"Okay, enough of that." Hydra glared at him. "Every once in a while we have group meetings where we talk about issues involving our community and other topics necessary. We have teachers who care for our few children, butchers, seamstresses, mechanics, cooks—just about anything you would find in a small town."

"Where does all of the food and everything come from?" I asked.

"We have livestock and fields of orchards and gardens that are all tended to daily. Every so often a few are assigned to go get supplies from nearby stores and factories that have long been shut down. We make good use of everything we get. Nothing goes to waste."

"I see."

"During the day we all tend to our tasks, but in the evenings, usually sometime after dinner, we all relax and have some fun together. Some like to swim in the lake, sometimes we'll have a small fire, but mostly we just visit and enjoy the last hours of the day."

"Sounds nice."

"It is, you'll get to experience it with us tonight, if you like."

"Aidan?" Rowen stopped. "Would you like to come with me to fix some plumbing?"

"Yes, I'd like to learn about that."

"Okay." Rowen and Aidan looked to us.

"I'm going to introduce Ivory to a few more people, if she wants."

"That would be nice."

"We'll catch up with you later, then?" Rowen asked.

Hydra smiled as he leaned in to press his lips against hers. "Sure thing…bye," she said.

"Hydra? What was that thing you just did with Rowen? When you said goodbye?" I asked as she led me back through the cabins.

"It's called kissing."

"What is the purpose of it?"

"It's a sign of affection, to show someone you love them."

"Does everyone do it, or just you and Rowen?"

"Ivory, humans have been kissing since the beginning of time. It's a very normal and common thing."

"Really?"

"Yes."

"And how do you do it?"

"Like this..." She brought the back of her hand up to her lips and kissed it.

I practiced on the back of my hand, feeling silly.

Hydra laughed. "You should try kissing Aidan. It's a lot more fun doing it with someone else."

My heart fluttered thinking about touching Aidan's lips with my own.

I followed Hydra into a small cabin that smelled of fresh bread and clean linen. An older woman greeted us and embraced Hydra.

"Did you come to put Akela to work?"

"No, not today. I came to introduce her to Ivory," Hydra said.

"Oh, hello. I'm Lara," the woman said, reaching out to grasp my hand.

"Ivory and her partner, Aidan, joined us yesterday," Hydra explained.

"Wow. So, you're learning the ropes, huh?" She smiled at me. "Akela!"

A small girl with light brown stringy hair appeared from

behind a wall. She peered at me with big brown eyes, half her body still lingering behind the wall.

"Akela? Come see Ivory, she's new here."

Akela shuffled across the floor toward us, keeping her head down. "Hello."

I smiled. "Hi, Akela."

"Akela, would you like to show Ivory how to make your famous bread sometime?" Lara asked.

"Okay!" Her eyes brightened.

"I would like that very much." I was sure to keep my most polite smile.

"Is Cara out in the gardens?" Hydra asked Lara.

"Yes, she's been out there since early this morning, probably daydreaming, as usual."

"I think we'll try to catch up with her, but we'll be seeing you two again very soon."

I made it known that it was nice to meet both of them before following Hydra back outside.

"Akela is very sweet," I said. "How old is she?"

"She's four, and one of our youngest. She and her sister were both born here."

"How old is her sister?"

"Cara is fifteen. She loves to work in the orchards and gardens and would be out there all day if no one came to get her. I think you two will make good friends."

Flora's happy face drifted through my mind and I realized just how much I missed her. I recalled her words about not wanting to lose me, feeling sadness stir deep within. The reality that I would never see her again, along with my broken promise, was too hard to bear.

We walked out past the cabins into fields full of trees and maintained gardens. Hydra listed off a multitude of names, explaining who everyone was and what they did, but my senses were on overload. I was tantalized by the beauty of nature surrounding us, understanding completely how Cara could stay outside forever.

As we walked along row after row of trees, women with baskets waved to us. Hydra picked a plump golden apple and dropped it into the palm of my hand. I had just begun to examine the speckled fruit when we reached a girl with the same shade of hair as Akela's, the length of it pulled up into a rubber band. She wore jeans and a sleeveless green shirt with a pink sweatshirt haphazardly tied around her waist. I observed her reaching up into the trees, recognizing a familiar expression upon her face. It was a look I imagined I had when lost in my own world.

"Cara?" Hydra called.

Her eyes lit up at the sound of Hydra's voice. She tossed her apple into a basket and ran to us, giving Hydra a big hug.

"Hey!" Hydra laughed at her enthusiastic greeting. "I've brought someone for you to meet."

Cara looked at me with deep brown eyes. "Hello." She seemed genuinely happy to meet me.

We properly introduced ourselves while Hydra got distracted by a friend.

"You came here yesterday, right?" Cara asked. "With that boy?"

"Yes, his name is Aidan."

"Yeah, I saw you walking down from the hill. Were you rescued?"

"No, we escaped."

Her big eyes got even bigger. "Really? That must have been scary."

I nodded. "It was."

"So, how old are you?"

"Sixteen."

"I'm fifteen, but I'll be sixteen in a couple months. How old is...Aidan?"

"He's eighteen."

"Is he your lover?"

I had to think about it for a second. "Yes."

"You're lucky. He's really cute. My mom doesn't want me to have a partner until I'm seventeen."

"Oh."

She looked back to her basket. "Want to come pick some apples with me?"

"Yes."

I followed her to the tree and observed Cara's technique for a minute before reaching for my own apples.

"So, what was the institution like?" she asked.

I spent the next fifteen minutes explaining everything about it, from the strict schedule and the mother nurses, to the names of the students my age and what an average day was like. The memories made me realize just how awful the place was. I was grateful not to be there.

"So, boys and girls were in separate wings and you weren't even allowed to *look* at the opposite sex?" Cara stared at me in disbelief.

"Yes."

"How did you and Aidan work around that?"

I smiled, happy to tell her about our hidden love affair. By the time I'd finished explaining all about the stair meetings, cooking class, our closet romance and escape, Cara was hanging on my every word. She sighed, looking up into the trees.

"That's the most romantic thing I've ever heard. I wish I could have something like that."

"Are there any boys here that you are interested in?"

"Well, Talon's cute, but he's already got a ton of lovers. There's Shiloh and Oran; but Shiloh's a year younger than me and more like a brother, and Oran already has a partner who just happens to be one of my friends."

"There are no other boys our age?"

"There's a few more but none that I'm all that interested in, or who are interested in me." She paused. "You'll meet everybody."

"Ivory?" Hydra joined us with a pleased smile. "I'd like to introduce you to at least one more person before we meet back up with Aidan and Rowen."

"Alright." I looked to Cara.

"Maybe later we can spend some more time together? I want to meet Aidan, too."

I smiled with the sure feeling that I'd found a new friend. "That would be nice."

The last cabin Hydra took me to was quiet and calm with a bright shade of yellow on the walls. Hydra whispered a name I didn't recognize when Deidra appeared in front of us.

"Hello, Ivory. How are you feeling today?" she asked, smiling.

"Much better, thank you."

"Good." Deidra's eyes met Hydra's. "She's resting."

"How is she doing today?"

"Better, the contractions have calmed some."

"Good."

"Hydra?" A soft voice called from another room. "Is that you?"

I followed Hydra into a small bedroom where a pretty woman with silky dark brown hair lay. Her belly was big and round underneath an oversized floral shirt. I wondered what was wrong with her, then I was sad thinking how terrible it was that such a young beautiful girl could have such a horrific deformity.

The girl smiled up at us looking drained from her ailment, but happy to see visitors.

"Who's this?" she asked, giving me a warm smile.

I quickly introduced myself, trying not to stare at her stomach.

"I'm Kia. It's so nice to meet you." Her eyes traced my face and hair. "You're absolutely stunning."

"Thank you," I said, aware that I was blushing.

"Kia is eight months pregnant," Hydra explained.

I nodded, assuming that that was the name of her ailment.

"Do you know what that means?" Deidra inquired.

I shook my head, completely embarrassed.

"It means she's going to have a baby."

"Yep." Kia patted her bulbous stomach.

"There's a baby in here." Hydra pointed to it.

I frowned. "There is? That's why your stomach is so big?"

"Yes," Kia laughed. "I know…weird, isn't it?"

"How did you manage that?"

Kia, Deidra and Hydra all burst into a fit of laughter.

"We'll save that lesson for another day." Deidra said.

"There's a real, live baby in there?" I asked, still trying to wrap my head around the concept.

"Yes," Deidra said, "and he'll be in there for a few more weeks until he's born."

"How is he born?"

"Through the birth canal."

I raised an eyebrow.

"I'll explain all the technical stuff later," Hydra assured me.

"Oh, he's kicking!" Kia lifted her shirt up revealing stretched skin and a belly button that was turned inside out. "Look!"

Her belly squirmed and jiggled with a small jerking movement.

"Would you like to feel it?" she asked.

Thinking it would be impolite to decline, I nodded, then my hand was suddenly flat on her tummy. A strange little force knocked my palm, startling me. I jerked my hand away.

"He must like you," Kia smiled. "He doesn't kick for everybody."

I spent the rest of our visit staring at Kia's stomach trying to imagine what the baby actually looked like inside. My imagination ran away with me until Hydra led us out to the lake that was surrounded by trees and sparkling in the sun. A small wooden plank led out to the water, and I noticed a thick rope dangling from a large branch hanging above. Footprints littered the surrounding mud as we walked along the edge, both of us taking in the beauty and tranquility of the environment.

"Ivory, look!" Hydra pointed out to the water where two birds floated along content as could be. I was fascinated by the small creatures, staring in awe at all of their quirky movements. They were the only living animals I'd ever seen—besides the bugs.

"That's Adam and Eve. They're our ducks."

"Ducks, yes. I remember learning about their species. So, one's a male and one's a female, right?"

"Yep, we've been waiting to see ducklings for a while." She paused. "Did they teach you anything about reproduction at the institution?"

"We were taught about how animals are bred and how they multiply, but nothing about humans at all."

She nodded, as if expecting my answer. "Well, I can try to explain to you how it works, if you want? I think it's important for you to know about your body."

"Alright."

We sauntered around the lake as Hydra did her best to clarify how a female's body functions and why, which I partly understood. Then she went on to explain how babies were made and how they were born—which terrified me. By the end of our conversation I was stunned, shocked, mortified, embarrassed and unsure of what to do with myself. It was the most confusing and disturbing thing I'd ever heard.

Hydra giggled at seeing how unglued I was. "You look worried. I'm sorry, did I say too much?"

"No! No, it's alright. I'm just trying to understand all of it."

"Look at it like a beautiful, natural thing. It's not supposed to be scary or weird."

"It's just a lot of information, that's all."

"I know… Should we go meet up with Rowen and Aidan now," a snicker burst from her lips, "or is that going to make it worse?"

"No, it's fine. I miss Aidan."

All I could think of was telling him about who I'd met and what I'd seen as we headed back toward the community. On our way through the cabins we spotted Rowen, Aidan, Talon and another boy with wavy blonde locks talking and laughing beside the creek. Aidan's eyes spotted mine and he beamed. I walked right up to him and gave him a big hug.

"Hi," he chuckled. "Where have you been?"

"All over the place."

"Me too."

Rowen introduced me to Oran, who was the blonde boy

Cara had told me about, then we all migrated to the big house. I helped Hydra prepare dinner, meeting a few girls in the process. Aidan, Rowen and the boys set the table and talked amongst themselves, peeking in every so often to see if anything needed to be done. Somehow they ended up being more of a hindrance than help. Talon harassed Rayne with a dishrag while Rowen would pop in to get a taste of food and Hydra. Aidan lingered in the doorway watching me intently. I knew he was enjoying the company around us just as much as I was. It was the best feeling in the world being amongst people who were cheery and upbeat, never scolding or condemning us for anything we did. They'd all welcomed us so freely, as if we'd been a part of their group forever, that I couldn't help but feel like I belonged. It was the only place I'd ever felt so complete besides Aidan's loving arms.

After an enjoyable dinner full of laughter and conversation, Aidan and I followed Rowen and Hydra out to the lake. Blankets and chairs littered the shore, along with a few people who were already taking advantage of the tranquil evening. We were welcomed with the same reaction Hydra and I had received in the orchards.

Rowen stopped at a patch of crushed grass where we settled, each of us getting situated in our own comforting ways. Hydra made a pillow of Rowen's stomach as he lay on his back, tucking his arms behind his head. Aidan and I sat side-by-side, so close we were touching. I was pleasantly surprised when he grabbed my hand and brought it up to his cheek. I smiled up into the sky that was beginning to change.

"What do you think of our community so far?" Rowen asked, turning his head to look at us.

"It's amazing," I said. "Everything seems so perfect."

"Well, it's not perfect, but it's a hell of a lot better than any institution."

"I agree," Aidan added, resting our clasped hands in his lap.

"So, what do you know of Oliver Driscoll?" Rowen asked.

"Oliver is the head of the institution we came from," Aidan said, a bit startled to hear the name.

"Do you know anything else about him?"

"No."

Rowen paused, staring up into the sky. "Have you heard of Geoff Driscoll?"

"No, is he related to Oliver?"

"Yes, they're brothers. Geoff is the one we've been trying to take down for years. He's built an entire corrupt army against the surviving civilians who want nothing more than to go on with their lives, as we do."

"That is the war you speak of?"

"Yes, but there's a lot more to it." Rowen sighed. "Before the plague hit, technology was advancing at an astounding rate and things that had been unbelievably impossible were being implemented. There was a man called Laris Windman who had been experimenting with machines and robots of sorts his entire life. He eventually created machines—human machines—that were incredibly lifelike. After he perfected and unveiled his first machine, there was a lot of controversy around whether or not these machines should be produced as functioning people. Some thought they would make great workers and be handy for whatever jobs humans didn't want to do, but others were very skeptical about intermingling humans and robots. They feared it would be too much of a liability and worried that things would get out of control—not to mention the fact that you literally could not tell the difference between humans and these machines—that's how lifelike they were.

"So, when the plague hit, after millions had been killed, Laris tried to convince the remaining government to produce his machines to fill in for all of the humans that were dying. They agreed and thousands of these machines were produced, but they were restricted to certain areas and only males and females of a narrow age range, about twenty-five years old, were created to replace the dying workforce. Things went well for about a year, until the plague nearly wiped out the human race, then production stopped and Laris died.

"Power-hungry Geoff worked within the factory that made Laris's machines and he wasted no time taking over the entire production, despite the human's objections. He figured out how to alter them and started mass-producing an army for himself. His goal is to create a perfect world of machines that he can dominate."

My head was spinning.

"If he wants a world of nothing but machines, then why are there still institutions?" Aidan asked.

"Nobody knows for sure, other than the fact that he likes to manipulate and control—human or robot. Some think Oliver convinced him to keep the institutions running for his own cause."

Worries about my siblings arose, causing my stomach to squirm. "So, when the children turn nineteen, where do they really go?"

Rowen paused, and after a few minutes I wondered if he was going to give me an answer. "They're sent to the city where he can do whatever he chooses with them. The men are turned into workers and slaves, some are brainwashed for war. The women work as maids and servants within his home and factory, and..."

"And what?"

Rowen looked to me, then Aidan, his demeanor apprehensive. "They're forced to reproduce with him."

I was sick thinking of Flora and all of the familiar faces I'd grown up with predestined to live a horrific life.

"Something has to be done." I demanded, emotions threatening to overcome. "We can't just let that happen to them." I took in a deep breath, closing my eyes to keep the world from spinning.

"Ivory," Hydra's soft voice attempted to calm my nerves, "it's okay."

Aidan wrapped his arms around me, nestling his face into my hair.

"Right now that's our main focus," Rowen added. "Shutting down all of the remaining institutions."

Rowen's words didn't help the heaviness in my chest, or the terrible visions that floated through my overactive mind.

"Are the mother nurses machines?" Aidan asked, clearly distressed.

"No, they're brainwashed—just as you were."

"And what of Geoff? Is he human?"

"Yes, but it's rumored that he's made modifications to himself."

"Where are all of the machines now? The ones Laris made?"

"Most of them are forced to live and work by Geoff's rules, just as the humans are. They maintain the city he lives in and do all of the dirty work, but there are actually quite a few who are helping us in the fight against him, more and more all the time. They've become our allies."

"Really? Are there any amongst the humans?" Aidan looked from person to person.

"No, it would be too risky."

"How do you know there are none in your community right now?"

"We scan everyone new with an internal imagery device that x-rays the arm—the only way to be able to tell the difference between human and robot."

Aidan's brow furrowed further. "But you didn't scan us?"

"There's no need to, all of the machines were built to appear at least twenty-five. There are no children machines."

A silence allowed my brain to soak up all of the spellbinding information as I noticed more and more people gathering around the lake. I watched the natural interaction between friends and lovers, still trying to wrap my mind around Laris's inventions. I couldn't fathom the idea of a robot looking and behaving exactly as a human. It was beyond my comprehension and completely unbelievable. A heavy feeling clenched at my abdomen while I thought about the fate of those in the institutions. I was more concerned about the mistreatment of humans and my siblings than the concept of the machines.

A fit of laughter broke my trance. I looked to the lake to see Talon in nothing but long shorts and Rayne in even less. I averted my eyes for a second before finding myself staring at them again, mesmerized. Besides my own, I had never seen another human body unclothed. I looked to Aidan who was just as uncomfortable by the sight as I was. He was trying, even harder than I, not to look.

"Is there a reason they're not wearing any clothes?" I whispered.

Hydra giggled. "You're lucky they're wearing bathing suits."

"You mean, underclothes?"

"No, bathing suits are what we wear to go swimming. They might look similar to underclothes, but they're different."

I widened my eyes, thinking I would never find myself wearing one. I watched Talon and Rayne play, splashing each other and laughing uncontrollably. They embraced, locking lips the way Hydra and Rowen had, only with their mouths open. My face burned. I swiftly looked away, not able to handle the raw intimate scene in front of me. I was glad when Aidan broke the silence.

"What is the difference between Geoff's and Laris's robots?" he asked, still intrigued by the subject. "You said they were altered?"

Rowen sat up to face us, sitting in a cross-legged position. Hydra rested her head in his lap.

"Both robots have the same basis—they're basically humans with mechanical parts. Their skeletal structure and part of the brain is machine, but they have all of the major organs, nerves, blood, muscle, tissue—everything we have, only it is made of synthetic material. They are even self aware, with emotions and feelings. They all look different; have individual personalities and a variety of characteristics, just as we do. They are all immune from disease and sickness, but Laris's robots can in fact die, they are still fragile as far as accidents, deep wounds or gunshots are concerned.

"Geoff's machines are built to withstand just about anything—physically and emotionally—they are specifically designed for war. They have built-in bulletproof armor enclosed within their torso, making the heart completely impenetrable. He also reprogrammed their bodies to be able to function without blood. If their blood is completely drained, the machine takes over."

"So, they are impossible to kill?"

"With guns alone, yes. Unfortunately, most of our weapons are still primitive, but we've managed to figure out what works and what doesn't throughout the years."

"Do humans stand a chance?" I asked.

"In the very beginning we were in hiding, completely unprepared and unsure of what to do. Geoff made so many machines that they overpowered us and he was unstoppable. After he sent thousands of machines out to hunt us down we started to fight back. It took many years and lots of innovative tactics, but with the help of our allies and new strategy, we are closer than ever to taking Geoff down."

"Good," I stated, with a little too much enthusiasm.

"I know what I've told you is upsetting, but I think it's important for both of you to be informed. You shouldn't have to be kept in the dark about what's really going on. We *will* win this war and take our world back."

I tried as best I could to be optimistic, but the shock and fear kept pulling me back. I was completely overloaded, unable to process any more and was relieved when Rowen was distracted by a friend who came over to greet him.

"Are you okay?" Hydra asked, her eyes sympathetic.

I nodded, unsure if I really was.

Aidan ran a hand over my hair and looked deep into my eyes, his face just as depressed as I knew mine was. I opened my mouth to ask if he wanted to go for a walk, when a cheerful Cara bounced in front of us.

"Hi, Ivory," she beamed, appearing excited to see me. Her smile slowly faded when she took in our expressions. "Am I interrupting something?"

"No, we were talking, but we're done now."

I introduced Aidan to Cara and vice versa,

"Want to come spend time with us by the boulders?" She pointed toward the thicket near the lake. "Everybody wants to meet you."

The last thing in the world I wanted to do was meet more new people, but I couldn't turn down Cara. "That would be nice," I said.

We followed her into thick brush beside the lake. A well-worn rocky path welcomed us and I realized that it was the same path that led to the rope I had seen dangling above the water earlier. The sky had turned a deep shade of pink, casting a warm haze over everything in sight. My eyes took in the unusual illusion, allowing my brain to rest for a few short minutes. I strained to follow along with Cara's chatter until we reached a clearing where a cluster of multiple gigantic rocks sat littered with scantily clad teenagers.

"Cara!" A dark haired girl wearing a small top and tiny shorts approached us. "Is this who you were talking about?"

"Yeah, this is Aidan and Ivory."

"Hi, I'm Phina."

"She's my best friend," Cara said as she wrapped an arm around Phina's shoulder.

"Hey, Aidan!" Oran came out of nowhere with a girl at his side. "This is my partner, Spira."

I found myself in a blur, meeting and greeting several friendly faces that all seemed more than happy to meet me. The notion was comforting, though my head began to ache, more strained than it had been minutes before. I leaned on Aidan as he conversed with a couple of the boys, observing all of the activity around us. A few partners sat resting on the rocks, some of them kissing and touching in ways I had never seen, others just simply content to be next to each other. I watched as kids chased each other around in fits of laughter, teasing and taunting one another with words and friendly play. Phina and a boy named Cai stood close, gazing at each other intently. All of the behavior I was witnessing was ab-

solutely prohibited within the institution's walls. And now…
I couldn't be cheerful when so many children were being mis-
treated and forced to live dreary lives. It wasn't right or fair.

Aidan must have sensed my mood, because within minutes he'd said goodbye and we were walking back down the
path from which we came. Before we could get too far, he
stopped and looked me over.

"Are you alright?"

"No," I confessed, "I don't feel very well. I'm overwhelmed."

"I am too… Do you want to go back to the house?"

"Not yet, let's go for a walk first. I just want to talk with
you."

Aidan took my hand as the light from the sky began to
fade even further. We broke through the trees and saw more
people around the lake, their laughter and joyous talk filled
the crisp evening air. I led us to the orchards through an open
grass field where the planets were just beginning to emerge.
We reached the shadows of apple trees and sat at the base of
a hearty trunk. I nestled up to Aidan in the crook of his arm,
once again appreciating the fact that I had him. Being alone
with my love was just what I needed.

"What do you think of everything?" I asked, truly needing
to know.

Aidan took a while to answer, his hand encompassing
mine. "I'm scared. I didn't think things were anywhere near
this complex. I'm still trying to understand it all."

"Me too, I just feel so sad for all of our siblings. We have
to save Flora, she means so much to me. I can't bear to think
that something terrible might happen to her."

"Well, the good thing is that most of them still have a few
years. I'm sure they'll be rescued long before they're sent off.

It sounds like the war might even be over before that."

"But what if it isn't? What if these machines come and attack us?"

"Rowen said earlier today that all of the men and some of the women are trained in survival and war tactics. They know how to defend themselves and keep safe, otherwise they wouldn't be here."

My mind went into fear mode. "But what if they come looking for us and the community is found?"

"They won't, we're safe here."

"How do you know?"

"I asked Rowen about it today. He said the mother nurses fear Oliver and that they probably won't even tell him we're missing. Even if they did, he wouldn't waste his time searching by ground—the technology is way more advanced than that. In any case, we're safe now."

I frowned. "What technology?"

Aidan sighed. "I don't want to scramble your brain any further."

"I want to know."

He hesitated. "Supposedly, every baby that is born in a hospital or facility is implanted with a tracking chip in the cerebrum, so they can keep an eye on us and find us if need be."

My heart pounded. "There's a chip in my head?"

"Yes."

I pressed my face into my hands, horrified.

"Ivory… Ivory, it's alright, they obviously don't do anything, otherwise we'd know."

My gut wrenched. "How is it that they can't find us?"

"There are blocking devices planted all around the community, making it impossible for the chips to be seen. And just to be on the safe side, Rowen said anything electronic or anything that could create a signal or frequency isn't allowed in the community. They want to be sure not to attract any unwanted attention to themselves."

I didn't know whether to be glad or distressed. "Is there anything else I should know, before I have a nervous breakdown?"

Aidan chuckled. "No." He wrapped his arms tightly around me. "It's going to be alright."

I let his warmth relax me, focusing on nothing but our contact and the sound of his breath.

"What did you learn today?" he asked.

My adventures of the day seemed so far away as I tried my best to remember all that I had wanted to share with him.

"I learned about babies and reproduction."

"You did?"

"Yes, I got to feel a baby inside a stomach."

I explained all about Kia and her baby, the little kicks I felt and how strange it was, then I told him the short and as non-embarrassing-as-possible version of how babies are made, getting more questions than I knew what to do with. I shared my encounters with Akela, meeting Cara and seeing Adam and Eve, then listened to Aidan describe most of his day. By the time he was finished I was feeling much better, distracted by lighter subjects that were surprisingly soothing. Thoughts of the kiss I had learned of drifted through my mind, causing my body to tingle. I hadn't yet decided exactly how I was going to explain that one.

"What do you think of these bathing suits?" he asked. "Strange, aren't they?"

I laughed. "Yes. It seems so inappropriate; but most of the kids were wearing them like it was nothing."

Aidan paused. "I wouldn't mind seeing you in one."

I gasped, then giggled, my face burning with heat. "Well, don't get your hopes up. I'm *never* going to put one of those things on. I'd be better off naked."

"I wouldn't mind that either."

I turned to face him, trying not to laugh but failing miserably. "Aidan!"

He laughed even harder, attempting to look innocent through the smile. "I'm being honest."

I shook my head, laughing right along with him. As we stared at each other in the rising moonlight, I decided to reveal my last lesson.

"Do you want to see what else I learned today?"

"Yes."

I leaned in and planted a kiss on his lips, just as I had practiced.

He looked stunned, then grinned. "What was that?"

"A kiss."

"Kiss. I like that."

"Me too," I said, just before giving him another.

rebirth

*T*he hot afternoon sun beat down on my fragile skin, never failing to burn the fair pigment. I wiped the dirt from my hands onto my jeans, then pulled my hair into a high ponytail as I looked up into the bright blue sky. My work in the gardens was done for the day, so I headed toward the apple orchards where Cara always waited. She stood in the shade of foliage; her basket toppling over it was so full.

"Ivory, your poor skin!" Her brows wrinkled. "Why aren't you wearing your long sleeves?" She glanced at the shirt tied around my waist.

"I got too hot."

"You have to cover yourself."

I ignored her, looking to the basket. "Are you ready?"

"Yep."

We each grabbed a handle then hauled the basket swinging between us through the cabins, stopping by each and every one to drop off a delivery. Cara chatted as she always did while I kept an ear open, listening for Aidan's distinct voice. I peered toward Talon's cabin, then looked to the big house and out toward the lake, but he was nowhere to be seen. Figuring he was still out in the training fields, I gave Cara my all, letting her drag me into her room when we reached her cabin. She threw clothes at me, gossiping about boys and the latest couples when Akela came in to join us. She crawled onto the bed behind me, taking my hair into her small hands.

"Akeelaa," Cara moaned, "can't you find something *else* to do? We were talking."

"You always get to play with Ivory. It's *my* turn."

"How was your lesson today, Akela?" I asked.

"Good, I got to paint!"

"Neat."

"It's drying, want to see it?" She poked her head around to see my face.

"I would love to."

Akela took my hand and led me to the kitchen where a rectangle mess of colors sat on the counter.

"It's beautiful."

"I made it for you."

"You are a thoughtful girl, Akela. But why don't you give this one to your mom? I think she needs a new piece of art."

She nodded. "Yeah, that would be good. Want to see my room?"

"Of course!"

I followed a bouncing Akela to the small pink room she

showed me nearly every day, though she never seemed to remember. Dolls, tea sets and art filled the space to capacity, making it known to everyone who entered that it was as "all girl" as you could get. I sat at the tiny hand-painted table in the center of the room while Akela poured me some pretend tea.

"Here, you can wear this hat." She placed an oversized vintage hat on my head, then placed one on her own.

"Thank you."

We giggled and sipped tea, talking amongst ourselves and her dolls until Cara stepped into the room.

"Ivory? We should finish our delivery."

"Alright." I turned to Akela, gently placing my hat on one of the dolls. "I'll see you later?"

She gave me a big hug. "Are you coming to teach tomorrow?"

"Yes, I am."

"Yay!" She jumped up and down, making me laugh. "You can help me paint some more pictures!"

The smile Akela consistently put on my face stayed with me as we delivered the rest of the apples. Once finished, we stopped by the creek near the house and watched the water trickle by. Phina joined us on her way back from tending to the livestock, her tan skin even browner from a full day in the sun.

"Oh, it's so hot." She gathered her dark hair in a mass, then waved a hand over the nape of her neck. "Guess who came to see me at lunch today?"

Cara grinned. "Cai?"

"No, Talon."

I frowned. "That's strange."

"Yeah, especially since Rayne just left him."

"What did he say?" Cara asked.

"He was being flirty. I didn't know what to do."

"You should go after him!" Cara stated. "He's single now, and apparently interested in you."

"What about Cai?"

"He's taking too long to make a move, maybe if you..."

My mind zoned out. I could only handle so much of their frivolous chatter. After a life of not being able to talk so much, I'd been conditioned to use my voice only when necessary. I didn't understand talking to talk, which seemed to be the thing to do as a teenager in the outside world.

My eyes drifted back to the water when a pair of strong arms embraced me from behind. Cara and Phina's jabbering ended immediately. I turned to see a smiling Aidan, along with Cai, Talon, Oran and Shiloh.

He planted a kiss on my lips before looking into my eyes. I couldn't help but feel shy with everyone around. It was still difficult for me to show affection outside of our room.

"How was the rest of training?" I asked, catching my breath.

"Good. I want to tell you about it."

He frowned, glancing down at my arms. "Ivory, you're burned."

I looked up at him with innocent eyes.

"Come on, let's get you out of the sun."

Aidan led me to the house where Hydra was folding mounds of laundry in the upstairs living room. He broke a small piece from one of two aloe plants, then had me sit on the couch where he gently applied the jelly goo to my arms.

"Ivory, you've got to protect your skin," Hydra warned.

"I know." I scanned Aidan's perfectly toned skin. "Why don't you get burned?"

He smirked. "I'm immune."

"That's not fair."

"It's a good thing you're working indoors tomorrow."

Rayne walked into the room from the kitchen looking solemn. She joined Hydra on the floor and grabbed a handful of clothes. They talked amongst themselves while Aidan finished slathering up my arms.

"Tell me about training," I said.

"Well, we did this—"

"Aidan!" Rowen walked in with a smile and a glass of water. "Are you up to helping me move that freezer?"

"Sure."

We gave each other a knowing grin, both of us all too aware of the fact that it was impossible to have a conversation out in the open.

Aidan stood, kissed me on the forehead, then left with Rowen as I joined Hydra and Rayne on the floor. The best part about the community, I had learned, was that there was never a dull moment.

✧ ✧ ✧

After a filling supper, Aidan and I joined our friends and new-found family out by the lake where we laughed and talked with everyone about the day's events. Akela had made a habit of sitting in my lap while the other small children danced around us whenever they weren't chasing bugs or playing in the water. Every once in a while we'd join the kids our age by the boulders, though it was clear we were both more comfortable out in the grass with everyone else.

The community had quickly become a new home for Aidan and I as we slowly adapted to their way of life, learning how to live all over again. We were both extremely happy, having made friends with nearly everyone and having a purpose the way we'd never experienced before. We contributed to the community in our own unique ways and were learning skills and talents about ourselves we didn't know existed. It was almost as if we were being reborn into a new and beautiful world, one that wholly accepted us just the way we were.

The reality of the war and my beloved friend Flora were never far from my mind, though the morbid images and worries had faded. I found comfort in the faith Rowen had for the men on their current missions. The fact that something was actually being done about it made it easier to go on.

Once the temperature had dropped and the sky darkened, everyone began to migrate in for the night. Aidan and I wandered to our room, both of us worn out from a long day in the sun. I giggled as he fell onto the bed, groaning with an arm over his forehead.

"I'm so tired."

I crawled over him, getting a sweet grin and look of admiration. He kissed me on the nose then I settled in beside him eager to talk about the day.

"Tell me what you started to tell me earlier?" I asked.

He brightened, instantly looking more awake. "We had a test today, to show how well we're doing and what level we're at—I did everything perfectly. Dryst says I have expert skills and they're all impressed with how quickly I've learned."

"That's great." I smiled, not expecting anything less. I'd already been hearing from others about how well he was doing.

"He says I'm as good as some of their best fighters and asked if I would ever consider going on a mission."

"What kind of a mission?"

"To take down an institution, possibly ours. Rowen said my memory of the tunnels would give them a great advantage."

My stomach sank. "No! I don't want—"

"It would be a good thing, Ivory. I would be helping to fight this war and rescuing others."

I sat up, disturbed by the news. "Why would you want to risk killing yourself after all that we've been through? We're together, safe and everything is good; why do you want to ruin that?"

"I don't." Aidan grabbed my hand. "Please don't be upset, it's only an idea. If I were chosen to go, it would not be for a long time from now."

"I'm going wherever you are, so if you do go, I'm going with you."

"No, Ivory."

"Yes, Aidan."

"I don't want you getting hurt," he said, looking intently into my eyes.

"Then I'll start training with you," I said.

"No."

"Yes."

We stared each other down.

"It wouldn't be a bad thing for me to learn how to defend myself, anyway," I admitted.

"You're not going out there."

"Then, neither are you." I cracked a smile.

"Alright, you win," he said, finally smiling with me.

"I *am* proud of you." I leaned over to gently kiss him, getting a full on kiss in return. We'd learned through practice and observation how to kiss in many different ways, though it was all still new. The sensations he had always invoked from within me had become increasingly intense, leaving me even more clueless as to what to do with these sensations.

I sat up, twisting my hair into a bun as a diversion.

Aidan's eyes scanned my body, stirring the butterflies already swirling.

"Are you working with Talon tomorrow?" I asked.

"Yes, we're going to maintain a few cabins and work on building a table."

"Is Talon interested in Phina?"

"I don't know. I think he's looking for a distraction."

"But doesn't he already have another lover? Isn't that why Rayne doesn't want to be with him anymore?" I realized I was starting to sound like Cara.

"Yes, and yes. I don't understand this multiple partner business. Why would anyone want to be with more than one person? It doesn't seem right. I don't understand Talon at all."

"Have you talked to him about it?"

"Yes, he sees things completely different than I do. I think he's deranged." He said it with so much seriousness it made me laugh.

"He *is* deranged. I'm still upset with him for showing you those magazines."

"He did it with good intentions. Besides, I had to learn somewhere."

I gave him a cynical glare. "Now, you know more about female anatomy than I do."

"That's not a bad thing."

I playfully pushed him, starting a wrestling match. We giggled and played until we were both too tired to move.

✧ ✧ ✧

Three little voices somehow managed to fill the entire multi-colored school cabin as I herded Akela, Hane and Fleur to storytime corner. A colorful round rug made for soft seating as they plopped down from bouncing, all three of them eventually getting settled. They harassed each other for a few minutes, arguing about who had the best seat, then helped me pick out a story about a fish. I sat in a chair above them, carefully opening and displaying each and every page while the students did their best to pay attention. Fleur picked her nose, Hane asked how the fish talked and Akela twirled a strand of hair around her finger shushing Hane in the process. I tried my hardest not to burst into laughter.

When storytime was over, Kia took my place and sang an animated song with hand gestures and clapping sounds. The children sang and laughed along while I tended to Fin, the newest addition to our family. He was the tiniest human I'd ever seen with round chubby cheeks and soft fuzzy hair. His little coos and smiles always melted my heart, so I made it a point to visit him at least once a day.

Fin and I took a small walk to the other school cabin, which held a variety of bigger children, even children my age who had decided to continue with their schooling. I was greeted by nearly everyone as we wandered around the room, observing children reading and scrawling in notebooks. I had a fascination with the setting, never getting over how open and communicative teachers and students were. Nobody was being scolded, looked down upon or punished, and the most amazing part of all was that you could ask questions—any question your brain could conjure. Everyone was taught at their own individual level, learning all of the basic subjects and whatever else they chose, and their curriculum wasn't warped or altered in any way as it had been in the institution. I had been tempted to try out the unrestricted teaching techniques, though Aidan and I had both made the decision to be done with our formal education. I had more of a desire to teach than to be taught, and Aidan was interested in anything and everything that didn't have to do with sitting in a class-room.

After getting plenty of attention from my fellow peers, Fin and I headed back to his mother and I left a little early with a stack of drawings and paintings created for me daily by Akela, Hane and Fleur. Our room had become a work of art in itself with dozens of little creations covering the walls. The sight always put a smile on my face.

I hung the new additions, changed my shirt, then went outside for a quiet walk. I found the need to zone out every so often, to unwind and gather my thoughts. The fact that I could, for the first time in my life, was enjoyable in itself.

My fingers grazed rough bark as my shoes crushed long dry grass. I stopped to finger leaves and smell tiny flowers, ex-amining every little detail around me. Sometimes I would imag-ine that Aidan and I were alone in our own little world again—just he, nature and me. Visions of our future were al-ways wonderful. I daydreamed about what life could be like for the world, our community and for mankind in general, every-one at peace and joyous. It didn't seem so impossible to me.

I stopped to observe intricately entangled branches when the sound of splashing water caught my attention. Thinking it was a little early to be swimming, I looked through the thicket to see Talon, Oran and Aidan laughing and playing in the sparkling lake. My heart skipped a few beats at the sight of Aidan's bare chest—it was the first time I'd ever seen him without a shirt on. I took a step closer, turning all of my at-tention toward his flawless, glistening skin. Every line and arc intrigued me and I found myself unable to look away. His body was perfect, exuding pure masculinity. Feelings I had grown accustomed to stirred. I fantasized about Aidan, his lean body and how much I wanted to touch it.

I watched as he ran his fingers through his hair, revealing even more muscle that flexed with every movement. He splashed Talon, then backed away, the water receding at his hips. I realized when he took a step further that he was completely naked. I looked away, embarrassed. Part of me was curious, though the other part knew better. I took one last glance, getting a good look at his appealing behind, then walked back along the path. The feelings my little escapade had created stayed with me all the way to my room.

I wasn't sure if it was because of the scene I had stumbled upon at the lake or the perpetual allure between us, but throughout the entire evening our attraction for one another was electric. We touched every second possible, gazed at each other through dinner, then took a walk on our own instead of joining everyone else at the lake.

With hands intertwined we strolled along the tree line, both of us in a frisky and playful mood. We'd described most of our day when I decided to tell him about my espionage.

"I was watching you today."

"When?"

"At the lake."

"And, you saw everything?"

I laughed. "No. I wasn't looking *that* hard."

"You can if you want to."

"When did you start swimming naked?"

"You *were* looking hard enough." He didn't seem to mind and we both started laughing.

I playfully rammed into him. "Aidaaannn…"

"Nobody was around. We were just taking a break," he said, putting his arm around my back.

"I don't want you doing that around other girls."

He grinned. "You don't want anyone else to see me?"

"No, not the girls," I reddened.

"Awe, you're so adorable."

I pushed him away, then ran toward the orchards, but he soon caught me and I was attacked with tickles from behind. We fell into the tall grass and then Aidan pressed his lips against mine, giving me a long passionate kiss.

"I have something for you," he said, staring into my eyes with a look that made my heart melt.

"What?"

He sat up to dig into his pocket and pulled out a braided cord with a round pendant attached.

"A necklace." He said, setting it gently into my palm.

I sat up to inspect it.

"The pendant is made out of ivory."

I eyed the intricately detailed off-white circle, thinking it looked so dainty. Tiny dots and diamond shapes were skillfully carved through the material, creating a unique design, extremely detailed. Someone had gone through a lot of trouble to create the delicate piece.

"Thank you. It's beautiful."

"It's to remind you that I will love you with all of my heart forever, no matter what."

Tears came to my eyes as I looked into his, never feeling so special. I pulled the necklace to my chest, noticing the fit was perfect. It was just the right proportion for my small body. Aidan helped clasp it, then stared at me in wonderment.

"It looks great on you. I knew it would."

I gave him a long deep kiss, and we fell back into the grass together.

After several minutes of passionate kissing, I stared into his alluring eyes and ran a finger over his lips.

"Do you want to go back to our room?" I asked.

A look of surprise and knowing spread across his face as he said yes.

We walked hand-in-hand with an unspoken eagerness, avoiding distractions at all costs. Once in our room we snuggled ourselves into a cocoon of covers, tenderly nuzzling and cuddling as we always did—but this time felt different. I gave in to the feelings exploding within me. I allowed myself to let go in a way that I never had before.

We kissed long and deep in the nearly dark room, unaware of anything but the chemistry going on between us. I boldly inched my hand up his shirt, grazing the soft skin over his chest and back. Aidan's breath grew heavy, his warm hand going from my hair and arm, down to my waist and hip where he pulled my shirt up to caress and awaken the skin. My stomach fluttered wildly as sensations stirred beyond my control and soon I found my own breath growing rapid. Piece by piece our clothes slowly made their way off as we took our sweet time exploring skin we'd never seen or touched.

Aidan planted tender little kisses all over my body, cherishing every single inch of me. I pulled him to my lips for a hungry kiss while the last traces of clothing fell away in a storm of passion. The reality of our bodies against each other with no clothing between us made my heart pound, and an overwhelming wave of love for Aidan surged throughout my entire being. I looked deep into his adoring eyes. I had never felt so complete, so beautiful, so perfectly matched with another person.

I couldn't imagine anything better until Aidan took us to the next level, our bodies melding together in a perfect embrace. My heart burst with overwhelming joy as we became one, bonding deeper in every way possible. Our love carried us away into the night until the euphoric feeling we'd created rendered us both completely useless. Shaky and trembling, Aidan nuzzled his face against mine, whispering how much he loved me before closing his tired eyes. I held onto the moment for as long as I could, eventually letting the warmth our tangled bodies created lull me into blissful sleep.

transformation

Sweat beaded from my forehead as my lungs strained to capture every bit of oxygen in the cool morning air. I picked up my pace, only a few steps behind Aidan who never struggled with our daily jogging routine. He turned and jogged backward, teasing me to go faster with a smirk that succeeded in making me smile and provided the boost I needed.

We finished our laps around the perimeter of the community, then headed to the training fields to do push-ups and crunches.

It was my first official day of training, after Aidan had talked me into it, offering to teach me himself since there wasn't a current group being taught. I had an inkling he was more excited about spending the day with me than the actual training, but I knew he was also looking forward to showing me everything that he'd been taught. I think he realized, too, that it would be a good thing for me to be as fit and strong as possible. Who knew what the future might hold? I'd begun to run and exercise with him every day. I wanted to get into shape and push my body in ways I never had before. Even though the physical routines always seemed to exhaust me, I was already noticing a huge difference. I'd gained some weight, along with a little muscle definition and was enjoying my new physique.

As we rested, passing a water bottle back and forth, Aidan dug into the black backpack he'd been carrying during our run. He pulled out a gun of some kind, along with hundreds of little bright pink balls. My eyes widened at the sight of the gun and I began to wonder what I'd gotten myself into.

Aidan laughed seeing my expression. "Don't worry. It's just a paintball gun—for practice."

"Oh." I couldn't take my eyes off of it.

"But before we do that we need to go over some of the basics." He took one last drink of water, then set the bottle down. "If this community were ever attacked I want you to run. Run as far and as fast as you can into the woods without worrying about anything else. Just so you know, the main weapon storage is in the old garage attached to the house. Some of the cabins have a weapon or two for their own personal self-defense, but anything that you would ever need to defend yourself is in that garage."

I sighed, reminded of just how serious life outside our wonderful community was. "Alright."

"I'll show you where everything is and what everything looks like tomorrow. Right now I'm just going to explain the three most effective weapons for fighting the machines. There are two main types of guns used—the laser and taser. The laser guns primarily burn whatever they touch. It won't stop the machines completely, but it will slow them down and do major damage. You want to aim the laser at their limbs or neck."

I grimaced.

"The tasers emit an electrical charge that short circuits the machine. The downside is that you have to be somewhat close in order for it to work, and it takes a few shots for them to completely shut down."

"Am I supposed to remember all of this?"

Aidan smiled. "No, we'll go over all of it again quite a few times."

"Good."

"Aside from the guns are the E-M grenades, which are your best bet because they're like mini bombs that scramble the machines with an electromagnetic pulse, causing them to malfunction completely—then it blows them to pieces. You can easily wipe out more than just one machine at a time, but you have to have a good throwing arm and some aim, so we're going to practice a few techniques that will prepare you for some of these weapons."

I hesitated, not prepared in the least bit to even think about handling weapons.

"You probably won't ever need to use any of them but it's good for you to learn, just in case. Who knows, you might have to save *me* someday."

I gave him a half smile, my brain was still trying to focus on the complex subject. "Have you used any of the weapons?"

"Yes, I've used all of them. But there's a *lot* of training involved before you even get close to firing any of the real weapons. That's why we're using this gun for practice, to get you started." He dropped the tiny balls into a reservoir.

"What do the machines use?"

"Standard military weapons. They don't use anything fancy because there's no need to."

"So they use bullets?"

"Most of the time, yes."

Aidan stood, holding his hand out to help me up. He guided me to a place in the field that was marked with lines, pointing out the wooden targets strategically placed ahead of us in the distance. After explaining all about how the paintball gun worked, Aidan showed me how to aim and shoot. I flinched when the gun went off as paint splattered directly in the center of the target he was aiming for. Thinking it didn't look too difficult, I finally took the gun in my hands and examined it before practicing my aim. Aidan stood behind me and helped steady the gun while I pulled the trigger for the first time. I chuckled with amusement. The concept was suddenly thrilling and I was excited to try again. I shot blasts of pink paint all over the place, never once hitting a target.

Frustrated, I handed the gun back to Aidan. "How did you do that? You made it look so easy."

"Don't worry, you'll get it eventually. Try it closer."

I spent the next two hours learning how to aim and fire a weapon. I shot from a variety of distances, finally making a target, then learned how to fire lying, kneeling, walking and running. By the time we'd finished for a lunch break, I was tired.

We settled underneath the shade of trees playfully tossing bags of snacks back and forth. When the food was gone, Aidan wrapped his arms around me and we rested, enjoying each other's company and the beautiful sunny day. Neither one of us wanted to get back to work but we eventually did, tickling each other as a motivation.

During the latter half of my training, I learned that my throwing skills were terrible. Aidan had me throw some white balls with red stitching as far off into the distance as possible until my arm felt like it was going to fall off. I couldn't hit a target if my life depended on it, and the little distance I could throw seemed to get worse as the day progressed. We ended up tossing the ball back and forth as another form of exercise, which I liked much better. Any kind of training that had to do with staring into Aidan's eyes was more than good enough for me. When I finally got the hang of aiming the ball into Aidan's hands, he stood by the targets in a silly stance that got me laughing.

"What are you doing?" I asked.

"Throw it at me, just like we were doing."

I threw it to him, watching it veer to the left, but he caught it anyway.

"Just pretend like the targets aren't even here." He rolled it back to me and I picked it up again. I succeeded in throwing it right to him a couple times, then he stepped back a few paces.

"That's not fair."

"Just try it."

I failed miserably. Aidan picked up the ball, tossed it up, then caught it. He smirked at me.

"Imagine that I'm a big, bad machine..." He started toward me. "And I'm going to get you!"

Realizing he was coming to get me, I squealed and ran away from him. He quickly caught up to me as we ran into the fields, falling into the grass laughing. I pulled him in for a seductive kiss.

"That's not going to work on the machines."

"It might." I nudged his nose with mine. "I could just stun them with my kisses."

"Not if I have anything to do with it."

I slipped my hand down to Aidan's hip, one of his biggest tickle spots. He giggled, stopping my hand with his own when a sound startled both of us.

"Aidan!" An excited man's voice sounded from the distance. We listened intently, glued into each other's eyes.

"It's Talon." Aidan stood, looking all around. "There he is!" he said, reaching a hand down to help me up.

I brushed off my shirt as Talon ran up to us, out of breath.

"Hey." He panted, looking from me to Aidan.

"What's going on?" Aidan asked.

"Our men are back."

Aidan frowned. "The men who were at war?"

"Yeah, they just showed up. They're talking with Rowen right now."

"How many returned?" Aidan asked.

"Three."

"Are they alright?"

Talon shrugged. "Looked like it to me. We'll probably have a meeting tonight. Everyone wants to know what's going on."

Aidan's eyes looked to me with concern. I could tell from his expression that he was worried.

We fetched the backpack then headed to the community where everything felt different from a typically relaxed afternoon. More people than usual were outside of their cabins and a big group congregated in front of the house. I stayed close to Aidan as we lingered with Talon and a few other friends, all of them chatting about the soldiers that had come back. Rowen appeared with three tired men, now clean and showered. They meandered through the community, reminding me of the first time we'd gotten a tour, only he seemed to know them all very well. I watched as they laughed and joked, stopping to greet anyone who crossed their path. Before long, they met up with our group, smiling and shaking hands. I studied the strangers carefully, unsure of what to think of them.

One of them looked about thirty with an athletic build and long brown hair. His eyes were gentle and I could see immediately that he and Rowen were good friends.

The second one I observed was a little younger, about twenty-five, which made me skeptical. He had a curly blonde mop and timid green eyes. His skin was fair like mine; only his was dappled with freckles. I quickly sized him up, deciding he didn't look anything like a machine.

The third one I attempted to study was studying me right back. I looked to the ground and kept my eyes there until Rowen's happy voice called mine.

"Ivory, this is Halin, Sirion and Darius. We've all known each other for a very long time. They've been at war for quite a while now."

I smiled and nodded, trying my best not to look at Darius who was still fixed on me. Rowen introduced all of them to Aidan, while I finally got a good look at Darius. I guessed he was about eighteen, since his face and body still had a hint of adolescence. He was the same height as Aidan with dark, nearly black spiked-up hair and somewhat fair skin. His eyes were a deep blue and his lashes long. He was attractive and the only thing that came to my mind was how wild the girls of the community were going to go over him. I chuckled to myself, looking to Aidan who was glaring ever so slightly at Darius.

Dinner was alive with conversation and laughter, but Aidan wasn't very engaged. As we walked with everyone out toward the lake for a community meeting, I stopped, pulling him aside.

"Are you alright?" I asked, cupping his face in my hand. His eyes left mine, then met them again. "I'm just concerned about the war and what they have to say."

"It's going to be fine. If anything was urgent we would have known about it already, don't you think?"

"Yes…" He looked away again.

"Aidan, is there anything else?"

"I don't like the way Darius looks at you."

"It doesn't matter. You're the only one I desire." I kissed him. "Let's go swimming at our special place after the meeting."

He smiled at last. "Sounds good."

We walked to where everyone gathered in a big circle and sat close to Rowen and Hydra. It took a while for everybody to come together, but once they did there was a unique feeling of unity that was stronger than ever. The air was still warm and the sun hadn't yet disappeared, making for a pleasant evening amongst our large family.

"Thank you all for coming," Rowen said, looking around the circle. "As you know, Darius, Halin and Sirion have been at war for months. They've just come back today to join us for a while before going back out. I know you're all curious to know what's going on. From what I can tell, things are looking very good." I squeezed Aidan's hand, already feeling relieved. "But they're going to tell you for themselves."

Halin, the oldest, spoke first. "Our human armies have destroyed thousands more machines and are getting closer to the city every day. We're using bigger E-M bombs that completely wipe out all of their equipment and vehicles along with hundreds of machines at a time, giving us a great advantage. With the bigger bombs we're going to invade the city and try to get into Geoff's factories. His production has slowed tremendously, so we're taking advantage of the opportunity."

Multiple questions arose, and Halin took the time to answer each and every one of them.

Sirion eventually spoke up. "Humans are growing by the numbers and our armies are getting bigger. The Gretchen Institution has just recently been shut down and there is a group currently working on another. We think Geoff is withdrawing because he's losing control of the institutions and realizing that we're not going to back down."

A small cheer sounded from the group, along with another round of questions. Once they had been answered, Darius stated his bit, speaking of how they had brought more weapons back to the community for our use. Then, one of the most important questions I'd heard all evening came from Phina.

"Is there any bad news?"

Halin looked to Sirion, then Sirion looked to Darius. It was clear none of them wanted to give it.

"A community in the west hills was attacked. All but one were killed."

"And Geoff burned another institution to the ground to try to get us to surrender," Sirion added. "We managed to save a few of the children."

My stomach lurched with a terrible feeling.

"That's the worst of the bad news," Halin said.

"The best we can do is protect ourselves and keep our eyes and ears wide open," Rowen announced. "But for now we're all safe. Halin confirmed that there aren't any machines anywhere near here."

"That's true," he said.

The group had an in-depth conversation about all they had been told, and once it began to dissipate I felt positive about the state of the war and our safety. Aidan and I broke away from the crowd and disappeared into the dark trees. We carefully walked toward our secret place, as we talked about how we were feeling. I was glad when we reached the rocks beside our pool, ready to focus on anything other than the war.

I sat on one of many grey boulders, removing my shoes before standing to unbutton my pants. Aidan began to remove his own clothes as we smiled, eyeing each other in the twilight. Once completely naked, I hurried to the water, reluctantly stepping in. The lake took away all of my body heat causing me to convulse with deep jittery breathing. I watched with a giggle as Aidan got in right behind me, joking about how warm the water was. We embraced with a kiss as the cold liquid engulfed our naked bodies, making me shiver as it always did. Aidan's warmth was the only thing that kept me there, other than his sweet kisses and love that always made me forget just how cold I really was.

✧ ✧ ✧

I realized when I awoke first thing the next morning that my second day of training was going to be grueling. Every muscle in my arm, back and shoulder on the right ached with excruciating pain, no matter how big or little the movement. Aidan did his best to massage my aching muscles during our morning snuggle, but before I knew it, we were off on our daily run and I was in pain again. I tried my best to tolerate it as we did our exercises, then we practiced with the paintball gun and I finally made a decent target, despite my discomfort.

After lunch, instead of throwing the ball, we walked back to the house so Aidan could give me a tutorial on the real weapons. We went through the kitchen to the adjoining door where Aidan lifted a framed picture from the wall revealing two keys hanging from a ring. I was apprehensive.

"These are the keys to this door and the cabinets inside. They're hidden so that the children can't get to them."

I nodded, watching him unlock the door as the lights struggled to illuminate within. It was cold and dim with a musty smell that reminded me of the institution. My eyes took in row after row of metal cabinets, all of them a pasty light grey lining the large space to its maximum capacity.

"All of the cabinets are locked for safety," Aidan pointed out, attempting to open one for effect. "But they all have the same key, which is this small one."

I carefully eyed the keys, storing in my mind the memory of which was which for future reference.

Aidan unlocked one of the cabinets and uncovered small compact laser guns. Their design surprised me as they were made with shiny silver metal and well-defined curves. He took one out and handed it to me describing what little parts there were and exactly how to shoot it. I was glad when he took it back, still feeling completely unprepared.

The second cabinet opened held slightly bigger taser guns that were jet black and heavy. Feeling bold, I practiced holding one in the palm of my hand, thinking it was a lot less bulky than the paintball gun I'd been training with. Aidan went over all of the basic rules he'd already explained, reminding me how they each worked and where to shoot with them. He placed the taser back, then picked up another to examine while I wandered to a small counter space. Two rectangular-shaped devices sat in the open, seeming exposed. I frowned, wondering why they weren't safely tucked away like all of the others.

"What are these?" I asked, looking to Aidan who had just finished locking one of many taser cabinets. He eyed the gadgets on his way over and appeared just as puzzled as I was.

"Those are the imaging scanners." He picked one up to inspect it. "They must have brought more back because we only had one."

Intrigued, I picked one up myself, thinking they were neat. A large clear glass screen made up most of the device and a small comfortable handle tapered toward the bottom. A trigger was strategically placed just above the index finger, easily accessible when holding the handle. "Wow, it's light."

"Strange, isn't it?" He seemed to be trying to figure out how to use it.

"So, how are these used?"

"Rowen demonstrated it for us once..." A click sounded, then a tiny green light appeared on top.

"Is it on?"

"Yes."

I held out my forearm for experimentation, curious to see what it revealed. Aidan put the glass screen directly over my skin unveiling every single detail of anatomy within. My eyes widened. I stared intently into the window, completely shocked to see veins, muscle and bone in full color as if someone had cut my arm in half to look inside. I pulled my arm away and squeezed it, feeling a little disturbed. Aidan laughed at me.

"That has got to be one of the strangest things I've ever seen." I said, looking at the spot where the window had been. "You can see *everything*."

"They were originally invented for medical use."

"Put it on you," I grinned. "I want to see your insides."

"Alright." He put it over his skin and I barely had time to glance at it, seeing nothing but dark matter, when the scanner dropped to the floor shattering into pieces. I stared up at Aidan whose face had completely drained of color. He looked completely horrified, causing my insides to wrench.

"Aidan?"

He stared at his hands as if looking at them for the first time, when a commotion sounded from outside. Yelling and harsh male voices penetrated my ears. I struggled to make sense of what was going on. Aidan suddenly snapped out of his trance and opened one of the big metal boxes stored on the floor. He pocketed a few hand grenades into his baggy cargo pants then looked to me with very serious eyes.

"Stay here."

"But—"

"I mean it."

I watched him leave through the door to the kitchen, frightened beyond belief. I was still trying to understand what had happened with the imaging scanner when a voice somewhere in the distance caught my full attention.

"We're looking for the one called Aidan." My heart leapt into my throat. I rushed to the door, swung it open and ran down the stairs to the big sliding glass doors. What I saw left me breathless.

An army of men in black uniforms charged through the community, fully armed with guns pointed straight for anyone who got in their way. All of them had cold, blank expressions. They looked ready to kill at a second's notice.

The machines had arrived.

I opened the door to hear them still inquiring about Aidan as my heart pounded in my ears.

"What do you want with him?" Rowen asked, stepping up to confront them.

"The master has requested we retrieve him."

"He isn't here."

"If you fail to surrender him we will kill all of you and burn this place to the ground."

"You will either way."

"We will leave in peace with Aidan."

"I am here!"

"NO!" I screamed, realizing I'd voiced it out loud. Blinded by tears and adrenaline, I ran toward him as fast as I could until someone grabbed me from behind. Aidan's arms were forced behind his back and put into a hold, then they began to lead him away. I suddenly became aware of the fact that he was being taken from me.

"AIDAN! NO!" I screamed with fury, thrashing to get out of Rowen's tight clutch. "Let go of me!"

"They will kill you Ivory!" Rowen said.

"I don't care!" I managed to get out of Rowen's grip, running toward Aidan with everything I had. I caught up to him and the machines leading him, throwing myself onto him as an attempt to make them stop.

"Please, stop!" I cried. "Please!"

"Who is this?" one of the machines asked.

"Nobody." Aidan's voice was grave.

I looked into his sad eyes, painfully aware of the tears streaming down his face. It only made me cry harder. "Why?"

"Remove yourself!" they ordered, pointing their guns straight at me.

I hugged him tight, burying my face into his until a force ripped me off of him. Rowen and Talon had me in their grips as I cried in hysterics, helplessly watching Aidan disappear into the forest.

tribulation

I sobbed, curled up on the ground for what seemed like forever, my lungs convulsing from being overworked. My heart and spirit were crushed; my mind unable to think. Hydra and others tried their best to console me, but it was useless. My other half had been ripped away from me without any warning and for no apparent reason. I didn't understand any of it and the possibility that I might never see him again was unbearable. Without Aidan, there was nothing—but I wasn't ready to give up.

Drawing from lingering adrenaline, I clambered to my feet and walked back to the village where everyone was in the process of an upheaval. Rowen appeared to be helping everyone organize and get supplies together. I walked confidently toward him, my head pounding.

"Ivory..."

"Why didn't you fight back?" I yelled. "Why isn't anyone out there trying to save him?"

"We have to take care of the community first."

"No! He's out there somewhere with those things! We have to get him!"

"It's not that easy—"

"I don't care!"

"Ivory, I promise that as soon as we get everyone out of here we'll talk about going out to save him. Right now there are precious lives at stake."

Tears threatened my eyes. "His life isn't precious?"

"That's not what I meant."

"I'll go get him myself!" With that I headed to the house, my mission being to grab weapons from the garage. I had barely taken a step when Hydra stopped me.

"Ivory, let's go for a walk."

"No!"

"You need to calm down."

"I don't need to do anything!" I started toward the house again but Hydra wouldn't let up.

"What are you going to do?" she asked, her voice a little more stern. "You're going to go in there, grab weapons and then what? Are you going to walk all the way to the city by yourself?"

I avoided looking at her, trying to push away a sense of reason. "Yes."

"How are you going to get into the city? Do you think they will just let you in? Do you think Geoff is just going to let you walk through his doors?"

I looked into her eyes and burst into tears all over again. She embraced me and whispered that everything would be okay. I gathered myself together enough not to do something foolish.

Within a few hours nearly the entire community had packed up and left, heading north to the nearest neighboring community. I stayed with Talon, Rowen, Hydra, Darius, Halin, Oran and a handful of others who had decided to defend the camp and wait to see if any of the machines returned. It was sad watching everyone go; there were many tears. Nobody wanted to leave, though we all knew it was best for the time being.

After setting E-M bomb traps all along the perimeters in the last light of day, the remaining group sat in a circle near the lake for a much-needed meeting. The buildings not so far away sat empty and lifeless, causing the hole in my heart to grow even bigger. Without the laughter of children or the sound of happy friendly voices, the community wasn't a community at all. It was extremely depressing.

Rowen sighed heavily. He looked to me just before speaking.

"Okay, first of all, I want to know why the machines came here to begin with. What the hell does Geoff want with Aidan?"

"They found out they escaped," Talon stated.

"That's what I thought, but they didn't look twice at Ivory. Why would they take him and not her?"

"Maybe there are others ordered to come and get her?"

"That doesn't make any sense, but maybe."

"He's an idiot," Darius said. "He would do something like that."

"Alright, so what is he planning on doing with them? Punishing them for escaping? I mean, the whole thing just doesn't make any sense," Rowen said.

"Well, they knew he was here," I said. "So they obviously know about the escape."

"Yeah." Rowen placed a hand over his mouth, in deep thought. "What does he want with Aidan?" he mumbled.

I took a deep breath, remembering back to our last moments together in the garage. I had completely forgotten all about his reaction to the imaging scanner as the scene came back to me. Pictures of the scan over his arm, the way it shattered to the floor and his face, pale with terror, played over and over in my mind, then suddenly it hit me. I had known it from that very second, though I had subconsciously lied to myself, secretly hoping it was something else. I didn't want to believe it.

"Rowen?" I asked, weary from my realization. "What does it look like when you scan a machine with the imaging scanner?"

He frowned. "It's an intricate mass of machinery within synthetic muscle and veins. Why?"

"Is it dark?"

"Yes. It looks nearly black through the device."

I closed my eyes, cupping my face in my hands.

"Ivory?" he asked.

"When we were in the garage..." My voice shook. "We were playing with the device and..."

"And what?"

"It was dark...he dropped it." I could barely breathe.

Rowen's eyes widened. "No way. That's impossible."

"It is?" I asked with hope.

"He came to your institution when he was sixteen, right?"

I nodded.

"Why would Geoff make a child?"

The entire group was in silence, everyone shocked by the possible revelation.

"Oliver," Talon finally added.

"Yeah," Rowen said, nodding. "That's the only thing I can come up with. Oliver wanted a machine for his institution."

"Maybe they were thinking of infiltrating the schools with machines?" Talon offered.

"What if they already have?" Halin questioned.

"I doubt it. Aidan's probably a prototype."

"What if he's a spy?" Darius asked.

"He's not a spy!" I yelled, barely able to handle the conversation in itself. "He surrendered himself so that all of us could live!"

Rowen nodded, silently agreeing with me. "If Aidan really is a machine, he had no idea."

"Well, that would make perfect sense as to why Geoff wants him," Halin said. "He's his little toy."

Rowen suddenly looked alarmed. "Shit. We've got to go get him."

I wanted to strangle all of them for being so slow to the idea.

"If we don't, Geoff will destroy him."

I panicked. "What do you mean?"

"He'll download all of Aidan's information—his thoughts, memories, everything he knows about us. Everything we taught him. Then, they'll turn him into a killer or a slave of some kind."

"You mean, they'll erase him?" I asked.

"Yes, Geoff will reprogram him into whatever he wants and use the information against us."

"We can't let that happen!" I cried.

"Alright, well we need to thoroughly plan this out," Rowen said. "Who will stay and who will go?"

Our small group worked to devise a plan. A dangerous plan, but well worth it. Six people, including me were to set out first thing in the morning a few miles south. Our goal was to get to a small underground storage area, which held two stolen vehicles used only for emergency situations. From there we were to travel just outside the city to meet up with a community of soldiers who could give us more information about the current situation and supply us with more equipment. The general plan was to disguise ourselves as machines to get into the city, then break up into pairs and slip our way throughout the factories and main buildings to find Aidan. I was scared, knowing absolutely nothing about the technical world that existed beyond. Not only that but the possibility of being killed or getting caught was extremely high. I realized the odds were against us, but all I could do was hope. If I allowed my distressed mind to take over, I was useless. I told myself I would stay strong and be the person Aidan needed me to be. He was all that mattered.

When everyone split up to prepare for the impending journey, I sat alone looking out at the dark rippling water. A cool breeze chilled my body as I hugged my knees to my chest thinking Aidan should have been right there beside me. Tears fell slowly and softly while I tried to comprehend everything. I was numb, unable to register half of what I'd heard and seen throughout the traumatic day. Worst of all, I couldn't help but wonder if everything Aidan and I had experienced was all just a lie. My heart screamed that it was all very real and true, but my brain wanted to pick it apart and explore whether or not it made any sense. Flashes of our precious memories and special moments danced through my head, making it even more difficult. I wept in the shadows until a body sat beside me.

"Ivory? Are you okay?" Hydra's gentle palm rubbed my back.

"Is everything just a lie?" I cried, wiping away the tears from my eyes. "Is everything we've ever experienced together false?"

"Of course not. Just because he's a machine doesn't mean he isn't real or that what you have with him is in any way compromised."

"So, it is all true?"

"Yes. It's as genuine as any relationship. The love you share with him is beautiful and nothing can take that away."

I sniffled, feeling at ease from her words.

"I don't think it matters what he is. He's a wonderful person and he loves you to death."

I sighed, thinking about the technicalities of our future. "So, does this mean he'll never grow old?"

"Yes, he'll stay the way he is forever."

"And we'll never be able to have kids?"

"No, machines don't reproduce."

I mulled over the ideas thinking I could live with all of it if only we could be together again.

"How do you feel about it?" Hydra asked with caution. "About him?"

"I don't love him any less. I'm just confused."

"I understand."

We sat in silence as the stars peeked out from a thin layer of clouds. I wondered where he was and what was happening to him, if he'd somehow escaped or if he was locked up someplace.

"Let's go in and get some rest." Hydra stood, brushing off her skirt before offering her hand. "You have a long day tomorrow."

There was no way I could go back to our room without Aidan. I already felt so empty without him.

"I think I'll stay here."

"Come inside, please?"

I gave in, taking her hand and following her footsteps into the house. Weapons and equipment littered the kitchen and hallways as the men prepared for the following day. They sorted and configured everything, being as thorough as possible. I snuggled into a blanket on the couch, watching all of the action until my body couldn't take it anymore. An agonizing restless sleep took me in its clutches, trapping me in darkness.

He squeezed his eyes shut, as if trying with all of his might to fight something, but there was nothing he could do about it—nothing at all. His flushed face was wrought with terror. An electric current jolted his entire body, causing him to scream out in pain. He was shocked again and again until his bloodshot eyes began to tear and blood dripped from his nose. He was weak, unable to handle any more. Needles and pointed tools poked him, digging their spires underneath the skin. He screamed out in protest once more—then it all stopped. He was blank and there was nothing left. A shell. He was dead. The skin fell away and a deadly machine emerged, its metal skeleton gleaming in white light....

I awoke panic stricken, covered in sweat, my heart hammering beneath my chest. Paranoia and anxiety kicked in full speed, starting my day with a terrible feeling. I sat up, recognizing that everyone was getting ready to go, walking in and out of the room in a hustle. The backpacks were packed, lined neatly along the living room wall and smells of breakfast registered. Rowen walked in, saw me half awake and gave a grin.

"You ready to head out?"

"I...think...so." I looked to the bags on the floor.

"Hydra packed your bag for you."

"Oh."

"There's breakfast in the kitchen. You better get some before it's all gone."

I nodded, still stuck somewhere between earth and my bad dream.

After forcing myself to eat, I got cleaned up and dressed into my sturdiest pair of jeans. I topped them with a black tank top and my small black hooded sweatshirt, then tied my hair into a loose knot. I laced up my ankle high boots then looked at my reflection one last time. I couldn't help but wonder what the day had in store for all of us.

Another round of goodbyes was almost more than I could handle, and seeing Hydra and Rowen part in tears made it a hundred times worse. I focused on making sure my backpack was adjusted just right as a distraction to keep myself from crumbling.

The sun lit the sky with a brilliant pink hue as all six of us—me, Talon, Darius, Dryst, Oran and Rowen—headed south through the trees. We each carried a backpack full of necessities and supplies that would last at least a week, along with a myriad of weapons for protection. I was the only one unarmed, but I was glad. The group was prepared and experienced enough to handle a battle if it came down to it and I definitely felt more than safe amongst the men I knew would protect me with their lives.

We trudged for what felt like hours, my backpack getting heavier by the minute and the sun getting hotter. I stripped my jacket off, tied it securely around my waist, then noticed a pair of prying eyes. Darius had turned to look at me. He smiled, scanned my body one more time, then went back to his focus on the terrain at his feet. I glared at his back, thinking I would tell him to keep to himself if he did it again.

The bad feelings that had lingered throughout the morning slowly faded with each and every step. I was optimistic, feeling like we were somehow getting closer to Aidan. Just the act of doing something was gratifying and my inner strength seemed to grow stronger—until Rowen dampened my high.

"Ivory." He caught up to me from behind, walking beside me as his boots crushed the foliage. "I need to talk to you about a couple of things."

"Alright."

"Once we get closer to the city there's a higher risk of being attacked. The community we're joining is more like a refuge for fighting soldiers, so we won't be completely safe. If we are ever attacked I need you to hide wherever you can and stay low to the ground."

I swallowed. "I understand."

"There will be bunkers and places for hiding, so when we get there I'll show you the best places to go. Also, I'm going to show you how to use our weapons, along with the weapons we'll be carrying inside the city."

My stomach knotted with nerves. "Is it hard to get into the city?"

"Yes, it's heavily guarded and only machines are able to get inside."

"How are we going to get in?"

"Every machine is stamped with a microscopic code within the iris of the eye for identification purposes. The only way to get into the city is to be scanned and recognized within the system, so we're going to use contact lenses that are implanted with codes we've taken from fallen machines."

"Contact lenses?"

"They're little clear circles that temporarily stick to your eye. It's old technology, but in this case they work."

"So, they won't be able to tell the difference?"

"No, I don't think so."

His hesitance rattled me.

"Don't worry, we'll go over every single detail once we get there." He paused. "And there's just one more thing I need to mention."

I waited, my gut now squirming uncontrollably.

"When we find Aidan there's a possibility that he could be erased, which means he wouldn't be the same person. If that's the case, it would be like the Aidan we knew died—he'd be completely gone."

My heart pounded. "Would it be possible to get him back somehow?"

He looked down. "No."

"Surely there has to be some way?"

"He'd be reprogrammed however Geoff wanted, completely brainwashed. He'd have no memories." He looked to me. "Ivory, do you understand what I'm telling you?"

"Yes." I fought back tears.

"He wouldn't know who you are." His eyes were strained with concern. "But there's still a good possibility that he hasn't been erased. I just wanted you to know, just in case, so that you understand if he's different."

I nodded, my mind already wandering. I imagined what it would be like if he didn't recognize me, didn't kiss me with his loving lips or hold me in his gentle arms. The thought made me sick to my stomach. I was unsure if I'd be able to handle it. I didn't want to lose all the memories we'd created, the love that we'd shared. I didn't want to start all over again or pretend like I didn't know as much as I did. I didn't want to lose us.

I tried as best I could not to fret or burst into tears during the remainder of our walk, but it was so hard.

We finally slowed, then stopped at a big natural shelf that sat quite a few feet above the ground below. Rowen circled the area for a couple of minutes, inspecting underneath the formation.

"This is it!" he yelled.

We joined him down below where roots and rocks protruded from the wave of unsettled earth. Rowen, Talon, Darius, Dryst and Oran dug into the dirt, eventually pulling open two big metal doors to a large black chamber. Curious, I walked to the square, looking in to see nothing but darkness. Talon and Rowen disappeared inside as I looked to the others who were covered in dirt.

"The vehicles are inside?" I asked.

"Yeah." Oran glanced at me. "They're really neat. Just wait till you see one."

I set my backpack down and untied the jacket from around my waist, taking the opportunity to rest on a fallen tree trunk. I was just about to fiddle with my hair when a soft purr sounded from the darkness. A spray of blue light illuminated the chamber, then the purr amplified and an object like nothing I'd ever seen before came gliding out.

It was astonishing. A huge mass of iridescent metallic panels sat before me curved into a sleek design that drew me into its beauty and class. I wanted to touch it, yet it looked so untouchable. It sat on four big wheels spaced at least eight feet apart on either side, the body compact and curved and just the right proportion. A big sheet of thick dark glass-like material wrapped around the top and sides, accenting the already attractive body. The lights emitted from the top, front and also from the back, giving it a surreal effect. It definitely looked like something that didn't belong in the world I had known.

I stared in awe, even more intrigued when the glass lifted and Rowen stepped out.

"They started well for being stuck in there forever," he said, looking excited. "We just need to let them sit in the sun for a few minutes, then we'll get going."

I walked to the vehicle, still intimidated by it.

Rowen laughed. "It's okay, you can touch it."

My fingers licked the cold dark body. "Why does it need to sit in the sun?"

"So it can charge. It's got solar paint."

I frowned. "Like solar panels?"

"Yes, but it's also hydrogen powered."

I peered at the interior, seeing more lights and instruments I didn't understand along with four seats—two in the front and two small ones in the back.

The second one drove out alongside the first one, then Talon appeared from underneath the window just as hyped as Rowen.

"How do you run it?" I asked.

"With the controls in there. It's normally voice activated but the computer's programmed to run in the city, so we control it manually."

Oran grinned. "It flies too."

"What?" I stared at him. "How?"

"The wheels fold in and it goes. It's incredible."

"Yeah, and..." Talon's words trailed off. I looked up at him, realizing all of the men were on full alert.

"Did you hear that?" Oran asked.

"Ssshhh." Rowen took a couple of steps, peering all around, when a loud repetitive sound pierced my ears, along with buzzes that came and went. I was immediately pulled down and behind the vehicle as Rowen drew his gun.

"They're here," he said, the tone in his voice critical.

I gasped. "What?"

"Come with me, stay low to the ground." Rowen crept along the vehicle then up the sharp hill of dirt, dragging me along with him. Bullets flew by all around us. When we got to the top we ran as fast as we could to a gathering of trees where we took shelter. Rowen struggled to catch his breath looking between the trees with his gun gripped tightly in his hands. My legs were shaky and my breath weak. I knew without a doubt I was a goner. Within seconds Talon joined us, just as breathless as we were.

"How many are there?" Rowen asked.

"I don't know, at least ten."

An explosion sounded in the distance, racing my heart even faster. I began to break down, crying and gasping for air.

"Ivory, breathe."

Another explosion jolted my body, along with five more.

"I think they got Oran," Talon said. "But Darius and Dryst are on their asses with E-Ms."

"Good, I'm going to stay with Ivory."

"Alright, I'll back you up." Talon disappeared, then a huge double explosion cracked throughout the sky.

"They destroyed the vehicles. Come on," he said, grabbing my arm.

We ran farther, attempting to get away from the shrapnel that flew through the smoky skies. My lungs burned as I was picked up and carried by Rowen. He stopped at a cluster of rocks and propped me up against the natural shelter.

"Ivory, I need you to get it together. Listen, you need to run as fast as you can away from the machines."

"I can't!"

"You have to."

"They'll shoot me!"

"If you go now they'll never see you, go!"

"No!"

"Shit! They're getting closer!"

I peered over the rock to see machines stomping our way, their weapons firing nonstop. A bomb exploded in the distance as I squeezed my eyes shut, opening them again to see the dark figures lying on the ground.

"They're getting them!" I yelled.

"They need my help. You're safe here for now—"

"Don't leave me!"

Talon appeared, running toward us. He dove behind the rocks and we all took cover.

"There's only a couple more machines left, but Oran's down and Darius is badly injured. We need to wipe out the last ones and get the hell out of here."

"Alright, Talon, let's go!"

"No!" I yelled. "Take me with you, I don't want to be left alone!"

I was pulled along, back toward the machines, then thrown behind a tree, as Talon and Rowen began to shoot. Bullets whizzed by as I was careful to keep every body part safely tucked behind the trunk.

"Yes!" Talon yelled, giving the impression of victory.

"There are two more!" Rowen said. "Let's get their asses!"

I watched as Talon activated and hurled a grenade. Within seconds there was another loud explosion. "I got them!"

I looked out into the smoky forest. I saw nothing but fire and destruction. Talon and Rowen broke free from their trees, cautiously taking a couple steps ahead. A machine emerged from the flames of Talon's latest grenade. I slipped back out of sight.

"How is that possible?" Talon asked. "I got him. I know I did."

"Throw another! Wait!"

A silence followed.

"Holy shit..."

"Ivory, run! Run the other way, now!" Rowen's voice scared me, but I was curious. Before leaping into the forest I looked back to see Aidan.

façade

My heart stopped.

I froze, trying to register exactly what I was seeing as he came closer and closer fully armed and completely enraged.

"Aidan!"

A pair of arms grabbed me from behind. "It's not him, Ivory!"

"Yes it is! It *is* him!"

"He'll kill you!"

"I don't care!"

Aidan lifted his gun and I was pulled to the ground. I scrambled to my feet and bolted toward him, unaware of the weapons pointed straight at me. I caught up to him unharmed, throwing my arms around him with all of my strength.

"Aidan..." I cried, happy just to be near him again. I nuzzled my face into his neck, telling myself I would never let go—no matter what.

"Get off of me!" I was suddenly thrown from his chest to the ground behind him, staring up in disbelief. He aimed his weapon toward Rowen and Talon, then began shooting at them.

"Aidan! Stop!" I stood and pulled on his arm. "They're our friends! Stop shooting them!"

He ignored me as I desperately tried to get him to stop, but he wouldn't let up. I looked toward the trees to see Talon drop to the ground.

"STOP!" I screamed. "You're hurting them!"

An electric sound sizzled from behind as Aidan dropped and hovered over me. He sat up and fired again, causing the sound to stop completely. The next thing I knew he was gripping my arm in a tight hold, leading me through the woods farther south.

"Where are we...?" My words halted at the sight of Dryst lying still and motionless on the ground. Dark red blood stained his body and the dirt surrounding him causing me to lose my breakfast. Aidan looked at me disapprovingly. I wiped my mouth, crying in shock and disbelief.

"Let's go." He tugged at my arm.

"What did you do? What have you done?"

"I eliminated the enemy."

"They're not the enemy!" I yelled through tears. "You killed our family!"

He kept marching, never missing a beat.

I sobbed uncontrollably, refusing to accept the idea that Rowen, Talon, Darius, Dryst, and Oran were dead.

"Where are we going?" I choked.

"The city."

"Why?"

"I've been ordered to bring you back."

"For what reason?"

"The master has requested your presence."

"No!" I jerked my hand out of his hold. "There is no master! And we're not going to the city. Aidan, listen to me..."

He grabbed my arm, forcing me to trudge on my tired feet.

"Stop!" I ordered. "Stop this, right now! You are not one of them! You're NOT!"

We reached two vehicles that were a slightly different version of the ones I had seen earlier, both of their doors wide open with lights aglow inside. He pushed me into the back of the vehicle then sat in the seat in front of me.

"Aidan! Please stop." I cried, finally realizing he truly was brainwashed and unlike anything close to the Aidan I had known.

"CT-1!" He ordered with frustration. "CT-1!"

The vehicle did not respond in any way as he frantically attempted to start it. I assumed it had been disabled from the E-M bombs detonated nearby. He got out, dragging me with him and tried the second vehicle. After getting the same reaction, he pulled me out and we continued.

I tried to grasp onto the emotions and thoughts rushing through my jumbled being feeling like my insides were in a tug of war. I had to decide which side I was on and which approach I was going to take.

"Aidan," I got in his way, nearly causing him to trip over me. "Look at me."

He was cold and unresponsive, his perfect face stuck in a scowl.

"Look at me, look into my eyes."

"Get away from me! You're making me angry!"

"Please, just look at me."

His eyes flickered to me for a second.

"I love you."

"You're insane!"

"You have to remember! This isn't who you really are! You were captured and brainwashed!" I struggled to recall any information that might snap him out of his trance, spewing out anything and everything that came to mind. He seemed to be getting angrier by the minute as I explained in no particular order all about the community and institution.

"...Remember how you saved me and we escaped through the tunnels? How we spent a few wonderful days in the wilderness together, just the two of us. You picked me berries and..."

"Be quiet!" he yelled.

"You gave me this necklace, remember?" I held it up from my neck. "You told me you'd love me forever and always, no matter what happened." Tears poured from my eyes. "Aidan, remember the first time we made love?"

"If you don't be quiet, I'm going to kill you!"

"Then KILL ME!" I screamed, getting one last surge of energy. "Because I'm not giving up until you remember!"

I watched his hand rise, then everything went black.

❖ ❖ ❖

My head pounded and pulsed with a pressure that was undeniable. I opened my eyes to see nothing but a blur of color going by with some kind of momentum. It took me a few minutes to realize I was being carried upside down, my hair nearly touching the ground below. I stiffened and wriggled, needing to get myself upright when the body slowed and grabbed hold of me. I was thrown to the ground so hard the wind was knocked out of my lungs, leaving me gasping. When my breath returned I took a minute to appreciate the solid earth supporting me, curling up into a comforting ball.

Two black boots appeared in front of my face. I looked up, past all of the gear and equipment to Aidan's glowering eyes.

"I'm not scared of you!" I yelled. "You can do whatever you want to me. I'm not giving up."

He picked me up and threw me over his shoulder as I screamed and kicked with all of my might.

"Let go of me! I don't need you to carry me! LET GO!"

I was set to my feet, then pulled along, my arm nearly raw from his unforgiving grip. Hopeless tears fell from my eyes as I questioned whether or not I would ever get my Aidan back. I grieved for what felt like forever, letting the tears consume me while the sky dimmed above. Every emotion humanly possible had affected me in one form or another, leaving me confused, frazzled and weak, questioning my sanity. I fantasized that it could have all been a bad dream and that I might wake up next to my sweet loving Aidan once again. I closed my eyes, wishing it to be true as hard as I could.

Pain jarred me back to terrible reality as I looked to the man who inflicted it. Everything about him looked the same, yet he was so different. His face was still as beautiful as always, free from injury or dirt. I wondered how he had remained unscathed after walking out of multiple explosions. I trailed down to his body where a vest full of equipment made him appear bulkier than he really was. Multiple guns and holsters of every kind clung to him, strapped over his shoulders, waist and legs. Every bit of it was jet black, making it hard to see what was what. The practical costume made him attractive as ever, despite his horrible persona.

My body deteriorated from trying to keep up with Aidan's long stride. I came to the conclusion that the only way I was going to get him to even remotely take me seriously was to get one of us into a vulnerable position.

I stopped, causing him to halt and look back at me. His frown softened ever so slightly at the sight of my big pleading eyes.

"I need to go to the bathroom."

He grunted. "Fine, go."

I stared at my arm, his knuckles still clenched on.

"I need privacy."

"Go here or hold it."

"At least let me have my arm!"

He let go and turned away, leaving no more than a foot between us. I pretended to pee, never really having to go in the first place. Any drop of liquid that had been in my body had apparently been used.

I stood, staring at his back for a second before letting him know I was done. He turned and reached for my arm but I pulled it away.

"Can we rest?" I asked.

"There's no stopping."

"Please?" I gave him my sad eyes again. "Just for a little while. I feel faint."

He looked as if he were contemplating it, then reached out to grab me.

"No! Please don't! That makes it worse." I forced tears to well in my eyes. "I just need to rest...please? Then we can con-tinue all night if you want."

He gave in, stomping over to a tree. "Fine."

I watched him take out a small device that he fiddled with, looking more and more frustrated when it didn't work. He sat at the base of the trunk, still trying to activate the object. I slowly walked toward him, falling to my knees in the dirt a few feet in front of him. He looked up at me then went back to his gadget.

"Do you have any water?" I asked.

He pulled a plastic bottle from his vest and handed it to me.

"Thank you." I opened the cap and gulped the liquid down, my burning throat temporarily relieved. After handing it back, he took a few sips then put it away.

"How long have you been under Geoff's command?" I asked, curious to know what his mind had been tricked into believing.

"That's classified information."

"What does he want with me?"

He frowned, never giving an answer.

Darkness began to envelop the forest, causing the temperature to drop considerably. I shivered, mad at myself for taking off the jacket that had once been tied around my waist.

"Is he going to kill me?"

Silence.

"Or turn me into a slave?" When he didn't respond I gave up, thinking of a different tactic. The cold made me shiver uncontrollably, but I added a little more to it for dramatic effect. Just as I had wanted, he looked up at me, annoyance written all over him.

"You humans are pathetic."

"Then your master is pathetic as well."

"He is anything but pathetic. He created everything that you see before you."

"Really? Is that what he's trained you to think? Because that's ridiculous!"

He shook his head. "You will be punished for such blasphemy."

"I'm already being punished!"

A silence engulfed us as I tried to stay focused on my plan. I shivered some more, getting his attention again.

"I'm so cold."

"Let's get walking."

"No, I need a few more minutes." I looked to him. "Will you hold me?"

"No."

"Please?"

"I'm not allowed contact with subjects."

"You've had contact all day." I held up my bruised arm, then sighed. "I won't tell anyone."

He shook his head but I crawled to him anyway. Without making eye contact I curled into his lap, ready to be pushed away at any second. When he didn't respond I allowed myself to relax against the warmth of his chest, content to be so close to the body that had once loved me. I rested my head just underneath his chin, closing my eyes to imagine he was his old self and we were merely resting together as we'd done a countless number of times. In the darkness it was like nothing had changed. He was so close, yet so far. I took a risk, looking up at his cold hard face before gently planting tiny kisses along his neck and jaw.

"Stop."

I did, going back to the fantasies in my head. Just before falling too deep, I grabbed his arm and hugged it close to me, nuzzling into him one last time.

I awoke after a deep sleep nestled soundly in Aidan's arms. The morning sunlight cast its bronze radiance all around us, lighting up the giant tree we'd leaned on in the night. He unknowingly held me tight on the cold hard ground as I stared up at his peaceful face that was for once free of tension. I never wanted him to wake, never wanted his terrible alternate self to return, so I lay as still as possible. The urge to graze his face with my fingers or kiss his soft ample lips was irresistible, but I managed to keep to myself. He eventually stirred, waking to the realization that he was holding me and quickly sat up. The scowl returned instantaneously.

"How did you do that?" he demanded.

I frowned. "Do what?"

"Get into my head?"

"What do you mean?"

"Never mind. Let's walk."

I pondered his question, figuring out that he must have had a dream about me—which meant that somehow, somewhere, the true Aidan was still alive.

"You're remembering!" I blurted out, getting to my feet. I took his face in my hands but he pushed them away. "I'm in your head because those are your memories. You have to pay attention to them. That is who you really are."

"You are ridiculous and your ideas are insane."

I ignored him, still reveling in this precious proof.

"I'll be glad to be rid of you."

"You love me," I stated, staring into his dark eyes. "And you know it."

"Let's go." He grabbed my arm but I yanked it back. "I can walk myself."

"If you run, I will kill you."

My legs screamed with every step I took, aching and sore from the past twenty-four hours. On top of that I had a bruised body from being thrown around so much and my arm was beginning to turn a deep shade of purple. I was so fatigued I could barely focus on anything, but somehow I kept it together in hopes that Aidan would start to remember more and more, then hopefully come to his senses. It was enough motivation to keep me going for a while.

I tried so hard to keep up with Aidan who was in every sense of the word tromping like a machine. He never tired, never took a break and never seemed to need anything but approval from his master. Feeling shaky and weaker than ever I stopped, calling out for him. He turned, gave me a frown, then stomped back to me.

"You are the most inefficient person I have ever met."

"How many people have you met?"

He thought about it for a second looking puzzled, then scowled. "What is it this time?" he said.

"I need to rest. I'm not an *efficient* machine like you." I wiped my brow, letting my hand linger there for a second. "So what's the plan here? Are we just going to walk until I die and you malfunction?"

His face was suddenly comical, surprising me. "A vehicle will be sent out to us."

"And then what?"

"We will go to the city."

"Why are you doing this?"

"I've been specifically ordered to."

"But why? Do you even know?"

"It doesn't matter."

"Why do you let him control you however he wants? You don't even know why you're doing what you're doing. Don't you wonder what you're serving for?"

"I'm privileged to serve at all."

I shook my head. "You're so much better than this."

He stared at me in silence.

"Don't you wonder how I know your name?"

"No."

"Or how I know that you have four curved lines on your right palm, instead of three."

He stared down at his hand with a frown.

"You're six feet tall, you have a thirty-two-inch waist, you wear size-eleven shoes and you'd rather your shirts fit a little tighter than looser."

A look of shock spread across his face. "You inspected me while I slept?"

I laughed. "I'm your lover. I know everything about you."

"I have no lovers, and I'd advise you keep your eyes to yourself."

"You're self-conscious of your ears, you get nervous when it rains, you love the feel of cotton, you hate the smell of metal—"

"Stop this nonsense."

"I'm not giving up on you, I know you're in there." I took a step closer. "You have to soften and allow yourself to feel. I can help you."

"I don't need anything from you but your cooperation, and if you don't stop with this madness I'll knock you out again."

I sighed, looking down at the pebbles spreckled throughout the tall grass.

"Let's go."

"Why are we even walking?" I asked, getting irritated. "If a vehicle really is coming then why don't we stay in one place and wait for it?"

It took him a second to answer. "That's not very productive."

I groaned with frustration, my growl echoing off the trees. "I hate this part of you!"

"Good. Let's walk."

"No!" I yelled, having had enough. "I'm staying right here! I don't care what you say!"

He took a few steps toward me but I backed away, turning and running as fast as I could with the little energy I had left. I nearly tripped over a cluster of rocks when he caught up to me and tackled me to the ground. He turned me over and grabbed my arms in a fit of rage.

"I've had enough of you!" he yelled, jerking my body to a sitting position.

I began to cry, once again feeling helpless and hopeless, when he gave me a look that stopped my tears. It was similar to the look I'd seen just before he'd dropped the imaging scanner—a look of shock and disbelief. The spell lasted half a second then he frowned, shaking his head.

"Aidan?"

He threw me over his shoulder where I was stuck jerking with every footstep.

The sun reached its highest point for the day, boiling the backside of my body. I bumped along against Aidan's strong shoulder feeling like a sack of potatoes. I'd surrendered to the fact that I was a prisoner, and that I had no other choice but to be dragged along by the warped machine that carried me. Even though I had absolutely no more energy to fight him, my brain still worked to come up with ways to get through. Deep inside I was still fighting with all of my might.

A surge of courage brought me out of my trance as I wearily requested he put me down. He stopped and attempted to set me to my feet, but I collapsed, falling to the dirt.

"Water?" I asked, my head dizzy from a swift rush of blood.

He handed the bottle to me and I quickly discovered that it only had a drop left. I hung my head, still trying to focus.

"I know it's up to me to save the both of us..." I mumbled. "But I don't know if I can do this anymore."

A deep purr sounded from above suddenly snapping me to consciousness. I looked up to see a vehicle descending from the sky hovering effortlessly as it slowly sunk to the ground.

"The vehicle has arrived."

A new wave of panic caused an adrenaline rush that got me to my feet. I hadn't prepared myself for anything other than Aidan and me alone in the wilderness. The thought of actually going to the city made me nauseous.

I threw myself onto Aidan in a last attempt to stop him pleading with everything I had.

"Please don't do this? Please? Let's just go home! We can start over and everything will be alright!"

He grabbed my arm but I resisted, pulling him right back with my weak hands.

"Aidan, don't! Don't do this! He's going to kill me! Please, don't!" I bawled, choking on tears. "You don't have to do this! We can go wherever we want! We don't have to go to the city!"

He'd easily managed to get me to the vehicle's wide open doors. I noticed it hadn't ever truly touched the ground, and was still hovering a few inches from the dirt.

"Get in!"

"No!" I cried, bracing myself on the cool panels. "Please?"

He crammed me into a back seat and strapped me down with a harness, then got into the front. The doors closed automatically.

"Hello, Aidan," a female voice sounded throughout the small space.

I frantically fumbled with my harness, jerking and pulling on the straps. My eyes went down to my lap where I found a button that released me, causing the voice to notice right away. She gave warning as I crawled into the front with Aidan.

"What are you doing?" he yelled. "Sit down!" He reassured the voice, then pulled a silver device out of a compartment, reaching for my hands. I pulled away and crawled onto his lap, taking his face in my hands to make him look into my eyes.

"You have to stop this, right now!" I demanded.

He grabbed both of my wrists, his face flushed with anger.

I yanked a hand out of his hold and slapped him across the face. "Snap out of it, Aidan! I need you! Wake up! It's me!"

Before he could completely restrain me I somehow managed to release my hands. I grabbed his face and pressed my lips against his, hoping that it would bring him back. Instead, he slapped me and threw me to the seat beside him. My hands were pulled tightly behind my back as I cried, my face smashed firmly into the seat.

"Aidan?" The voice inquired. "Destination CT-1?"

"Yes."

the city

The vehicle began its departure as the sensation of floating caused severe spasms within. If there had been food in my stomach it wouldn't have stayed there for long. I had the urge to grab a hold of something but the restraint that had been forced upon me made that impossible.

Aidan pulled on my arms, sitting me upright next to him on the seat, but I didn't look at him or speak a word. I was temporarily hypnotized by all of the tiny lights, screens and controls before me. An intricate puzzle of high-tech gadgets and gauges lined the entire front of the vehicle, along with an expansive window—the same window that flipped opened. I was alarmed to see that we were way up high, too high. The trees looked like tiny sticks and the land like a never-ending pattern of colors and shapes. I fought for air, jerking my head down to my lap with a promise to never look outside the vehicle again. After a few minutes I allowed myself to analyze the lights and controls again, noticing a circular symbol everywhere. It was on the flat colorful screens, buttons and knobs, and even had a place in the seats. I frowned, wondering what exactly it meant, when Aidan spoke up.

"I have no choice," he said, his voice a little less gruff than usual.

I finally looked to him, giving him my own scowl. His eyes were soft and if I hadn't known he was such a savage, merciless machine, I would have thought that maybe he was feeling bad about all that had happened.

"Yes, you do." I snapped. "You are your own person and you can do whatever you want. You don't have to live under Geoff's command, you just think you do because he wants you to."

A silence filled the space.

"What do these symbols represent?"

He hesitated. "It's the master's trademark."

I frowned. "What does it mean?"

"G.O.D."

I was silent for a while, staring at the circle, which contained one vertical line slightly to the left and a single horizontal line toward the bottom right. I went over the words a few times before realizing it was Geoff's initials stacked into one symbol. Fears of what would become of me started to surface.

"How long will it take to get to the city?"

"Twenty-four minutes and fifty-three seconds."

My heart began to race. "Are you going to take me directly to Geoff?"

He looked straight ahead with no answer.

"Please, don't? We can go anywhere else, but not there."

"I told you. That's not for me to decide."

"Well, you're an idiot!" I flew off the handle. "You're nothing but a stupid slave like all the others!"

"I am different."

"How?"

He looked to me. "That's classified."

I groaned with frustration. "If I could strangle you right now, I would!"

"That's why you're in restraints."

I steamed in my seat, not even caring about my fate if it couldn't be with the true Aidan. I stared at the profile of his face, tears threatening my eyes.

"I'm sorry," I said. "I'm so sorry I've failed you. I love you."

His eyes flickered toward me, but he didn't move or say a word.

The vehicle began its descent, reminding me that I was getting closer to doom. Curious, I glanced out the window, but this time didn't see trees. Tiny buildings of all different shapes and sizes littered the land, intermingled with flat grey lines. It looked like a massive three-dimensional grid in one ugly color. Movement caught my eye as little vehicles like ours floated along the grey lines, and if I squinted, I could see miniature dark figures.

Machines.

"Entering CT-1," The voice announced.

We descended even more, eventually reaching the same height as the tallest buildings. A sea of gleaming vehicles littered the blue sky, whizzing by left and right. I braced myself as best as I could with my legs, staring down at the detail below. Row after row of buildings seemed to go on forever in their plain grey shade, fading into the hazy brown horizon. There was no ornamentation or color except for black G.O.D. circles that stood out on the fronts of most buildings. I caught a glimpse of a swarm of soldiers marching in an organized square, when we were suddenly engulfed in darkness. Blue lights lit up rows of vehicles and dark slabs of cement. We glided through floors, finally turning into one of them where the vehicle came to a stop into an empty space.

"You have reached your destination."

The window and doors automatically flipped open letting in cold air. I shivered, hunching into myself before being pulled from my seat. Aidan's eyes were aglow with blue reflection as I stared up at him, silently pleading. He led me through the dark underground facility where dim orange lights barely lit the space. I observed numbers and symbols painted throughout the walls, thinking they played a part in some kind of organization. I looked ahead to see the only well lit area in the place where two sets of large red double doors sat. It dawned on me that that was where we were heading, and that I had one more chance.

"Aidan, please stop!" I wriggled to get away. "Don't do this!"

He grabbed my shoulders in a tight hold, forcing me to look at him. "Stop it! Stop this madness right now!" he yelled.

I slowly began to cry.

"You had better compose yourself before we go in there or he really *will* kill you!"

"I don't care! I don't care anymore! And neither do you!" I screamed. "Why don't you just kill me right here, right now? Do it! Kill me! I'd rather you do it than him! Come on! What are you afraid of?"

He grabbed a hold of me, dragging me toward the doors with his hand firmly covering my mouth. We reached the big red slabs where he spoke a few words and stared into a screen. Within seconds the doors opened, revealing walls of shiny, intricately designed wood paneling.

"Welcome, Aidan. Which floor?" the voice inquired.

He stepped in, carrying me along.

"One hundred seventy."

The doors closed and a whirring sound began as we moved upward. Aidan released me.

"Behave yourself."

"You really don't remember anything? You don't remember me? Us?"

He ignored me, staring straight ahead.

"What about the pictures in your head? Those weren't programmed into you. You've seen more, haven't you? I know you have!"

He looked to me. "Only because you've been incessantly harassing me!"

I paused for a moment, taking in a deep breath. A blurry reflection of my broken and battered self stared back at me in the glossy lacquered wood.

"Just be sure that you're doing the right thing," I said, still holding his attention. "If you feel like this is the best thing for you to do, than do it. But if there is any question in your mind that this somehow isn't right, please stop."

He looked down, giving me the impression that a tiny bit of emotion had broken through.

"I love you, Aidan, and I always will."

"I'm sorry." He looked to me, stirring up an ounce of hope. "But I am not the Aidan you speak of."

My heart sank, but I accepted what he had to say. "Alright."

We stood in silence as the box continued to rise, causing my hearing to muffle. I was numb again, feeling like nothing but a shell of myself, though I was rampant with emotion. Everything had been drained from me and I'd accepted defeat, unable to battle the war I'd already lost.

"Floor one hundred seventy." The box stopped then opened its doors revealing a huge spacious hallway gleaming with the same wood. A red carpet spread out before us all the way down to immense wooden double doors. Fancy cone-shaped lights evenly dotted both sides of the paneling, and upon the ceiling was a line of windows mirroring the carpet. Along the walls were pictures of the G.O.D. symbols, all alternating colors of red, black, grey and white. It was intimidating, but the most terrifying element of all was the armed machines lining the hallway on either side, evenly spaced just like the lights. They didn't move or make a sound as Aidan led me down the red carpet. It was so eerily quiet; I could hear my own pounding heartbeat.

When we reached the massive, ornately decorated doors, a machine stepped forward and scanned Aidan's eyes with a device that looked similar to the imaging scanner. The machine grabbed a hold of me, his grip much tighter than Aidan's, then watched as another helped Aidan remove all of his weapons. They checked the restraint holding me, patted my body down, then scanned me with a wand before I was handed back to Aidan. We stood as the machine stared down at the device he'd used to scan Aidan with, as if waiting for something.

"Send him in," it said.

The doors opened to a second set of double doors, then we were scanned again with tube-like blue rays that came out from the walls. I began to fret, more scared than I had ever been in my entire life.

"Aidan?"

He frowned, shaking his head at me.

"I'm scared."

The rays stopped, then a click released the doors in front of us. They opened to the biggest room I had ever seen.

The first thing that caught my eye were the windows looking out to the city below lining at least half of the oval-shaped room. A huge red circular carpet sat in the middle of the wooden floor with a dome of patterned windows above. Shiny wooden furniture the same shade of the paneling sat in clusters throughout, none of it the least bit inviting. I looked to the right, noticing the walls were blood red, to see a big desk with a large black flag above. This time, the G.O.D. symbol was bright white.

I swallowed, shifting my eyes toward the other side of the room to see a man walk out from the shadows.

His expression was aglow with a smirk as he lifted an auburn drink to his lips, leisurely stepping toward us with sparkling dark green eyes. I took him in as quickly as possible seeing well-proportioned features and a freshly shaven face. His hair was jet black and cut short, adding to his neatly groomed look. He wore a pair of black dress pants and a black jacket; its vee revealing a crisp white button-down shirt underneath. Everything about him looked artificial.

"Hello, Aidan." He gave a quick grin before his eyes burned into me. "Release her from the restraints."

"Yes, sir."

"Hello, Ivory." Geoff paused, scanning every part of my body as Aidan complied. My arms fell to the front, limp and weak.

"It's nice to finally meet you...in the flesh." He grinned. "In fact, I wouldn't mind seeing more of it."

I stiffened, feeling exposed.

He chuckled, walking over to the desk to set his drink down, then turned back to us. "I'm sorry, I'm being rude. You do know who I am, don't you?"

I focused on my breathing, not daring to make a sound.

"Geoff. Geoff Octavius Driscoll." He held his hand out for me to shake, but I kept my palm flat against my thigh.

"That's fine." He took his hand back. "I'm only trying to be civil." He reached his hand out to my face as I flinched, pulling back slightly. "You're easy on the eye, aren't you?" He tipped my chin up, then to the side. "I bet you're even more attractive when you're clean."

I relaxed when he drew his hand away, thankful that he hadn't taken it any further.

"What a waste." He shook his head. "We could have had beautiful children together."

I grimaced.

"Aidan, take her over toward the windows."

"Yes, sir." He led me over the red carpet, past the desk to the sheets of glass that displayed the ugly city. I stood motionless on the wooden floor as Aidan stood before me, waiting for his next order.

"Stay nearby," Geoff ordered him. "I'm going to need your assistance."

"Yes, sir." Aidan turned and stood against the wall, his face blank. I was glad he was standing in my line of vision, finding it a comfort in the unbearable situation.

Geoff sauntered over and glanced out the window for a minute before giving me his full attention. "He is beautiful, isn't he?" he asked, never leaving my eyes. "Aidan is perfect in every sense of the word. He's an original, the only one of his kind and the blueprint for all of my future creations. He's an ultimate machine, built with the structure and immunity of my army machines, but gifted with so much more. He was made to withstand any kind of disabling device, unaffected by weapons that cause my other machines to malfunction. I created him with more strength and sharper instincts, enhancing all of his senses beyond human capabilities. He's more lifelike than any machine that's ever been made, extremely bright, quick-witted, observant and very intelligent, with the ability and desire to learn.

"At first he was somewhat of a test subject, that's why I created him for the institution, so we could keep an eye on him and see how he responded amongst humans. He exceeded our wildest expectations, excelling in ways we did not foresee." He paused. "That was before we found out about you."

He circled around me, still sizing me up. "I didn't think my machines had the capacity to love, but Aidan proved me wrong. Somehow, he created that ability on his own."

I looked to Aidan noticing a puzzled frown upon his face.

"You really made an impact on my machine, and I'm flattered that you have such strong affection for my creation. It's just too bad none of it's real."

"It *is* real!" I heard myself say.

He chuckled. "Aidan has no idea who you are. Aidan? Do you know this girl?"

"No, sir."

Anger consumed me. "That's because you erased him and messed him up! He's been brainwashed!"

"I did nothing but give him life, a life well deserved to serve *me*. He was never meant to leave the institution walls, but you, you screwed everything all up!" His eyes flickered with fury. "Do you know how many questions you raised? You nearly destroyed my brother's entire institution!"

"An institution of lies!"

His nostrils flared. "I am doing them a favor, keeping them focused and in line, preparing them for a life to serve their master."

"You're abusing them!"

"Who are you to question me?" He commanded, his voice echoing off the glass before us. He scowled at me hard and long before looking away to his city. In an attempt to quietly compose himself he took in a deep breath then turned and glared down at me again.

"Foolish girl. You're going to pay for all of the trouble you've caused." He walked across the room to the desk, his fingers reaching beneath the surface. Within seconds a square rose from the floor, growing into a giant rectangle as it reached Geoff's height. He pulled a white handkerchief from his pants pocket then took something out of the rectangle.

My breath grew rapid. I wondered what exactly Geoff had in mind. A whip perhaps?

I looked to Aidan whose eyes hit mine for a split second before he went back to his blank, emotionless stature. I wondered if the conversation had impacted him enough to open up his heart to the truth.

"Aidan?" I whispered.

He looked to me once more, the fact that he was no longer ignoring me a relief.

Geoff returned carefully holding a small black gun within the white handkerchief, his fingers arranged in such a way that didn't allow contact with the weapon.

I nearly leapt out of my skin.

The reality of actually being killed shook me to the core, causing a widespread panic throughout every part of my frazzled being. I was suddenly in full on survival mode, scanning the room for an escape, but when I tried to move my legs they wouldn't budge.

"You see, Ivory..." Geoff announced, walking toward Aidan. "Love doesn't exist in this world, *my* world." He handed the gun to Aidan who accepted it without question, then tucked the white kerchief into his jacket. "And I'm going to show you why."

Geoff took a few steps back toward the desk, grabbed his drink, then walked to the center of the room, lifting the glass to his lips. I watched his Adam's apple bob as he swallowed, then he looked to me with an evil smirk.

"Aidan, stand before Ivory and prepare to fire."

"Yes, sir." His response knocked the wind out of me. He marched to where I stood, clicked the gun, then pointed it straight at my head.

"No!" I crumbled, falling to my knees. My body shook uncontrollably. Tears streaked my cheeks as I stared up at Aidan with pleading eyes. "Don't do this! I love you!" I begged. "You have to remember who you truly are! Don't let him do this to us!"

Geoff laughed. "What do you think of your love now, Ivory?"

I ignored him, my main focus Aidan's dilated pupils. He looked down the barrel of the gun, a wavering frown creasing his brow. I knew the machine didn't want to do it, which gave me hope. I told myself that maybe he'd grown some kind of feelings for me in the time I'd spent with him, realizing that if he had, that was all there was left.

"Please, I know you don't want to do this! You have a choice! Don't do it!"

"Kill her."

"No!" I screamed, my sobbing irrepressible. I stared up

into his conflicted eyes, knowing I was going to die any second. "Aidan..."

"Kill her!"

"I forgive you." I cried, never taking my eyes away from his. I squeezed my eyes shut, feeling my body trembling out of control as I prepared for pain and darkness.

When there was no shot, I looked up just in time to see Aidan turn the gun on Geoff.

"Aidan! What are you doing?" Fear strained his voice. "Kill her, now!"

"No."

"How dare you defy your master!"

"You are not my master!"

A euphoric rush of relief hit me like a drug, causing me to collapse to the floor.

"I am your creator, your God!" he yelled. "And you *will* listen to me, or I will destroy you just as I created you!"

"You will never harm another human or machine!" Aidan yelled, taking a few steps closer.

"You cannot kill me Aidan, I have altered myself. I'm just as strong as you are."

"You're weak."

The gun fired, its loud crack reverberating throughout the room along with the sound of Geoff's shattered glass. I looked up to see Geoff staring down at his red stained shirt, regaining his balance from being knocked a few steps back. My heart leapt as he looked to us with a smile spread across his face.

"You're going to have to do better than that."

Aidan lifted the gun that was still lingering in his hand and pulled the trigger, but all that sounded was a small clicking noise.

Geoff laughed. "I wasn't foolish enough to give you more than one bullet."

"I don't need bullets to kill you!" Aidan pounced on him, causing both of them to fall to the floor with a thud. I watched in horror as they struggled to overpower one another, throwing punches and inflicting pain. I worried for my lover's life, feeling totally and completely helpless.

Geoff slammed Aidan into the red carpet. Aidan fought to regain control, struggling to take his enemy down. They seemed to be equal in strength as Geoff had warned, causing me to panic all over again. I watched as Aidan took Geoff into a merciless chokehold, smashing him into the carpet with his knee firmly taking the place of his hand. He punched his face repeatedly as I looked away, unable to handle the violence. Groans and whimpers overwhelmed my ears along with the sound of flesh being beaten. I turned to glance back at the brawl when the desk came into view, along with a reminder of the square on the floor and what it held. I slowly crawled on shaky hands and knees, inching along the room toward the desk as Aidan and Geoff fought to the death. Aidan suddenly cried out, causing me to stop and see Geoff twisting his arm. I quickened my pace, noticing I was only half way there when Aidan kicked Geoff away. To my horror, Geoff started walking away from Aidan toward my side of the room. I stopped and froze instantly, seeing Aidan getting up to take him down again. Instead of going to me like I assumed he was, Geoff threw himself over his desk struggling to reach for something.

"No," I heard myself mutter, thinking he had the same idea I did, then suddenly Aidan began to scream.

He writhed and yelled with his hands over his ears as if to be in terrible pain. I looked all around, completely clueless as to what exactly was causing his discomfort. There was absolutely nothing that I could see.

"Aidan?" A wave of anxiety hit me as I wondered what whatever it was would do to him.

Geoff's smile returned, along with his composure. He slowly sauntered toward the middle of the room, enjoying Aidan's torture.

"You may be strong, but you're not invincible." He wiped the blood from his lip. "Every design has a flaw, every man a weakness."

"Stop it!" I yelled, my heart twisting seeing Aidan in so much pain. "What are you doing to him?"

Geoff ignored me, staring at Aidan who had fallen to his knees on the floor. "Ultra high frequencies don't feel too good, do they? You should crash in about..." He looked down at his watch. "Twenty seconds."

There was no way I was going to let that happen.

I crawled as fast as I could to the desk, staring up and underneath to try to find any kind of buttons—but there was nothing. Thinking there had to be some kind of hidden compartment, I patted every surface, noticing Geoff scanning the room for me. My hand grew shakier by the second as I kept my eyes on him, still pressing relentlessly. His eyes finally hit mine as the pressure from one of my fingers caused a small flap to lift. I fingered a button and pushed it, watching the square rise from the ground. Geoff started towards me but Aidan grabbed his leg, still cupping his ear with the other. I grabbed the first gun I saw in the small rack, then stood, aiming it straight for Geoff who had kicked Aidan away.

"You don't even know how to use that thing," he mused.

My fingers thumbed the trigger as my mind went over the information Aidan had once taught me. He was right, I didn't specifically know how to use that particular gun, but with a general knowledge, I'd figured it out. I clicked off the safety then pulled the trigger, watching tiny orange rays fly towards Geoff. He shouted out in pain as I did my best to aim straight for him.

"Stupid bitch!" He stormed for me in a fit of rage, his face red with heat. I frantically shot him over and over again until he forced the gun out of my hand and threw me across the floor. Pain registered as I collided with the hard surface, then a searing burning sensation hit my shoulder, making me cry out in agony. Geoff pulled the trigger again but Aidan rushed him, tackling him to the ground. The laser grazed my arm, causing even more unbearable pain. I writhed on the floor in a cold sweat. Dizziness threatened to take me into darkness until visions of Aidan malfunctioning snapped me back to reality. My focus went to the thrashing going on only a few feet away where Geoff pummeled a weak and struggling Aidan. He did his best to cope with the frequency and Geoff's attack all at the same time, quickly deteriorating between the two. I dragged myself across the floor, using my good arm to pull me to the gun rack, then grabbed what I recognized as the taser. The gun shook wildly in my grip as I aimed straight for Geoff's back and fired repeatedly. Electric bolts instantly stiffened his body, sending him to the floor where he was paralyzed, then completely lifeless.

Geoff was dead.

The only thing on my mind after taking Geoff down was disabling whatever was causing Aidan's suffering.

I scrambled to the desk, finding the secret compartment of buttons and pushed them, but nothing happened. Still holding the taser in my hand, I smashed the controls with the butt of the gun, then crawled over to Aidan who was still in pain.

"I don't know what to do!" I cried.

"Shoot it!" He yelled, still cupping his ears. "Shoot it!"

I hurried back to the desk and shot the broken button compartment, watching it spark and sizzle. Aidan finally relaxed on the floor, his hands dropping away from his ears. I crawled to him, running my hands over his battered face and body in a frenzy.

"Aidan?"

He opened his eyes and slowly sat up, getting a grasp on his bearings before taking me in his arms.

"Are you alright?" he asked, looking me over.

I nodded, completely forgetting about any pain as I gazed into his weary eyes. My Aidan was back. Happy tears poured down my cheeks.

"Ivory, you're bleeding." His words were panicked. "We have to get you help."

"I'm fine."

Guilt washed over his face and he began to crumble. "I'm sorry. I'm so sorry, for everything. I never meant to hurt you."

"It doesn't matter, I love you."

"I didn't mean any of it. I didn't know what I was doing."

"I know." I wiped the tears running down his face thinking of my only concern. "You're not going to change into a killing machine again, are you?"

"No, that program was weak. It began to fail a while ago."

Another question I was sure I already knew the answer to was eating at me. "Did you know you were a machine?"

"No, I found out with the imaging scanner."

I looked deep into his distressed eyes. "I don't want to lose you again."

He hesitated. "You don't care that I'm a machine?"

"I don't care what you are. I love you." I nestled myself into him, unaware of everything except the two of us. "Let's go home."

flight

"This isn't going to be easy." Aidan admitted, his words laced with anxiety. "We need to get through that hall and to the elevator. Are you able to walk?"

I looked up into his eyes. "Yes."

"We have to pretend that you're still a subject." His gaze fell to the floor.

"Alright." I cupped his face, bringing his eyes back to mine. "It's fine."

"I'm going to get you out of here one way or another, I promise."

Aidan stood, helping me up in the process. We walked past Geoff's limp body toward the main door where Aidan searched the wall for a switch. He quickly found the panel then looked to me.

"Are you ready?" he asked.

"I think so."

He stared long and hard into my eyes. "I love you."

With the touch of a button the doors opened, then we were getting scanned by blue rays again. Aidan grabbed a hold of my arm as I mustered up some tears, which wasn't too difficult considering the throbbing pain in my shoulder. I readied myself for a dramatic show just before we stepped out into the hall still lined with machines.

"No!" I cried. "Don't do this to me! Don't let him do this to me!" I sobbed with everything I had, jerking away from Aidan's hold.

The same machine that had confiscated Aidan's weapons took a hold of me, putting my arms in restraints once again. Aidan received every one of his firearms back without question, then I was back in his grip and we were walking down the red carpet towards the elevating box. I hoped we'd make it out of the hallway alive, doing my best to keep up the act.

"No!" I sobbed. "Don't do this!" Tears continued to flow as the red doors became closer, though they still seemed like an eternity away. My heart pounded with an uncontrollable terror that fueled the raw emotion circulating throughout my entire being. Just before we reached the doors I yanked myself away from Aidan, falling to my knees in front of one of the expressionless machines.

"Help me!" I pleaded, staring up at his cold face. "Don't let him do this!"

"Let's go!" Aidan's gruff voice temporarily returned as he pulled me to my feet to the solid double doors. The screen recognized his voice and code, then the doors were open and we were standing inside.

"Hello, Aidan. Which floor?"

"G-3."

The doors shut out the sight of the hallway and all of the machines, alleviating most of the anxiety that had been tearing me apart. I breathed, letting in a big breath of air as Aidan took off the restraints and hugged me close.

"I'm sorry," he said.

"I'm just glad we got out of there."

"It won't be long before they find out. We have to move quickly." He released me, then began unbuckling his loaded vest. "I need you to stay close to me."

"Alright," I said, watching him take the vest off, then set it on the floor. He pulled the black long-sleeved shirt off that had been underneath, then took off another vest of some kind, leaving him in nothing but a plain black t-shirt.

"I want you to put this on." Before I could ask why, he helped me take my tattered tank top off, then slipped the vest onto my torso. "It's a protective vest."

"But doesn't it look suspicious?" I asked, watching him adjust it to me as tightly as he could. "It's obvious that I'm wearing it."

"I don't care."

"Won't the machines question it?"

"They don't have the authority to question me." He slipped my tank top over the oversized vest. "If they make an issue out of it, I'll kill them."

He redressed and buckled the armed vest back on as my mind spun with the realization that we were still in grave danger. Aidan arranged my hair over the bulk of my shirt when the whir from the moving box suddenly changed.

"Floor twenty-three, going down."

"Clasp your hands behind your back." Aidan ordered, standing beside me to grab my arm once again. My heart began to race with anxiety as the box slowed, then eventually stopped. The doors opened, revealing two machines and a huge service room that reminded me of the big industrial kitchen at the institution. Pipes of all shapes and sized emerged from the tall ceiling and every wall I could see was grey. A sea of tables and workstations filled the entire room, along with what appeared to be civilians. There was no way of knowing if they were human or machine, but one thing was for sure—they were slaves.

The machines stepped in as the voice greeted them, then inquired which floor they were going to. Just before the doors closed, my eyes caught a sight that jarred me. A young woman stood next to one of the workstations wearing a grey dress similar to one of the mother nurses' uniforms, her belly big and round beneath the fabric. She was very pregnant, most likely with Geoff's child, I thought. I wanted to reach out to her, to all of them, to let them know that everything was going to be alright, and that they were now free to live their lives as they pleased. The desire to run into the room and announce that Geoff was dead was strong, but I wouldn't have dared try. My life would have ended instantly, along with Aidan's and possibly all of theirs. There was no way I was willing to risk any of that.

The doors shut and silence ensued, all but the sound of the box moving farther and farther down its shaft. The machines stood slightly in front and to the sides of us, looking forward in a blank stare as they always did. My gut squirmed with nerves. I watched them through my peripheral vision, sure to keep my head down to appear solemn. The box slowed again and just before it stopped, I watched them glance at each other ever so slightly.

Please just walk out of the box, just walk out of the box and don't look back....

"Floor twenty."

A dizzy spell came over me as the elevating box proceeded to decelerate. I leaned into Aidan's strong stance to regain my bearings then tried as best I could to compose myself. My wounds, the sensation of moving and an overflow of adrenaline was throwing every system in my body off, excluding the terrible incidents I'd been subjected to in the past couple of days. I was in every sense of the word a mess.

When the box finally stopped, my palms began to sweat. I watched as the machine's boots stepped out into a blank hallway, then the doors began to close again.

"G-3!" Aidan ordered.

"Ground level three."

"Are you alright?" He turned to me, holding my weight into his body.

"I'm getting weak." I admitted, thinking I had been getting weak for days.

"Once we get to a vehicle you can relax until we get home, then we're going to get you help."

Just the thought of being back home at the community warmed my heart with a comfort that was undeniable. I wanted more than anything to be there with Aidan and all of the wonderful people that made it what it was.

The box came to a halt with a slight jerk, then the doors opened to what appeared to be the exact same storage facility that we had arrived in.

"Come on." Aidan gently took my hand, looking in every direction as we swiftly walked down one of the endless rows of vehicles. We had walked quite a ways away from the elevating box doors, when he finally stopped and dropped my hand to search his vest. He pulled out a mini gadget with a screen that he tapped, his gaze moving back and forth from the device to the painted numbers above one of the vehicles. Within a couple of seconds the vehicle doors opened and a blue glow emanated from within.

"Hello, Aidan," the voice responded.

"Halt, traitor!"

My heart leapt into my throat, causing a severe wave of nauseous. I looked to see a small group of machines marching toward us from the big red doors, each of them pointing weapons directly at us.

"Get into the vehicle," Aidan instructed, his voice stern. He gently nudged me along as I walked to the vehicle, setting a foot in. I looked back to see him pulling out weapons and ammunition.

"What are you going to do?" I asked.

"I'm sending you home." He ducked in to speak to the voice. "OA-53."

"Destination OA-53. Please get into the vehicle."

"No!" I panicked, removing my foot. "I'm not leaving you."

"Get in, Ivory."

"No!"

"Right now! Get in!"

"Halt! Or we will shoot!"

Aidan turned to face the angry machines that were now only a few dozen feet away. He held a gun in each hand, pointed straight for them. I was sure to stay as close as I could to the open vehicle.

"Surrender your weapons." A machine ordered. "You will be severely punished and destroyed."

"Geoff is dead, there is no need to fight anymore. You are free to live as you choose."

"Prepare to fire."

"The war is over! There is no one left to report to!"

"The alternate master has been informed and wishes to disable you himself. Continue to resist and we will take matters into our own hands."

"Let her go and I will do as you say."

"No!" I yelled, walking before Aidan with determination. "You won't do this to me again!" He seemed to ignore me, though his arm did a good job of moving me out of the way and back behind him.

"She is to be destroyed as well."

"Then I will have to kill all of you."

"Fire!"

"No!" I wailed, hearing nothing but the sound of guns firing. I squeezed my eyes shut, ready to feel a bullet rip through my body at any second. Buzzes and clinks echoed throughout the facility as I became aware of Aidan's body still firmly standing in front of mine. The sound of marching boots thundered off the cement walls, along with even more deadly blasts. I knew we were dead, until a huge boom sounded from somewhere just above the structure. The cement beneath my feet shook, causing me to fall to my knees, then the lights flickered and blackness followed. The gunfire stopped and another boom vibrated the structure's walls. I was startled by the sensation of being rushed through the facility in someone's powerful hold.

"Aidan?"

"It's alright. I'm getting us out of here."

A loud siren pierced my ears, along with the sound of a message that repeated itself.

"Warning, city under attack. Warning, city under attack..."

We stopped, then I was leaned against a vehicle and a tiny square screen appeared floating in the blackness. Fingers blackened the light, then the vehicle doors opened. The blue light and female voice was suddenly appealing. Without words I was whisked inside, then Aidan got in and the doors closed.

"Disable remote access and vehicle network connection," Aidan stated.

"User Aidan, insufficient access privileges—request denied."

"Dammit!"

"Specify destination, please?"

"OA-53."

"Destination OA-53."

I felt the vehicle rise from the ground, then we were moving through blackness lit by bright blue lights. I looked to Aidan in the glow of lit up gadgets from the dash noticing he had been shot several times. His arm was bleeding where bullet holes had cut through the fabric and his vest was tattered and torn. Blood was running down his cheek where a bullet had just missed his face. I panicked.

"Aidan!" I scrambled to get a good look at him, tears falling freely from my eyes. "What did they do to you?"

"I'm alright."

"No, you're not," I cried, wiping the blood from his cheek. "You're bleeding."

"I'm fine. Did you get hit?"

"No."

"You scared me. I thought when you fell..." His words trailed off.

I sobbed into his chest, consumed by overwhelming concern for his well being. "Are you in pain?" I asked, frantically trying to search his body through the vest.

"I can take it."

I looked into his tired eyes letting emotion get the best of me. "Why did you do that?" I demanded. "You could have lied, or you could have gotten into the vehicle with me in the first place!"

"I'm sorry..."

"And why do you always insist on sacrificing yourself?"

"I wasn't really going to let them take me. I just wanted you to be safe."

We stared into each other's eyes until daylight poured in, blinding me momentarily. When my eyes adjusted I realized that we were well above the ground amongst billows of grey and black smoke.

"What's going on?" I asked, trying to get a glimpse of the city through the haze.

"I think the humans have finally gotten in."

"The war is truly over?"

"I hope so. I don't think Oliver is insane enough to try to build another empire."

I took a good look at Aidan in the daylight, trying to assess the damage that had been done. Unfortunately, most of it was concealed beneath his clothing, making it difficult to tell just had bad it was.

"Let me look at you." I tried to pull his sleeve up but his hand stopped mine.

"I'm fine. It's you I'm worried about."

"Won't the bullets damage you?" I asked.

"No, once they're taken out I'll heal just fine."

"How do you know?"

He gave me half a grin. "I'm special, remember?"

"That doesn't make me feel any better."

"I know." He gently hugged me as I relaxed in his arms, elated to finally be going home. I closed my eyes, reliving the day and events that were suddenly so far away. Everything that I had been through seemed surreal and insignificant as we drifted through the clouds. It was hard to believe any of it had really happened. All I could think about was getting back to our normal lives amongst our loving family at the community. I let my mind wander, imagining Aidan completely healthy and happy walking beside the lake with a great big smile. I saw Rowen and Hydra, Cara, and little Akela bouncing around in the grass with Fleur and Hane. Others who were dear to me walked in and out of the picture, then a voice startled me back to the real world.

"Vehicle being summoned for check-in."

"What does that mean?" I asked, looking up at Aidan who had just opened his eyes.

"Ignore command." He said.

"Request denied."

He sat up looking frustrated. "Bypass vehicle check-in. Proceed to destination OA-53."

"Request denied."

Aidan frantically fiddled with the controls as the vehicle began to descend. I braced myself.

"What is it doing?"

"It's going to a check-in at one of the entrances. All of the active vehicles are probably being searched."

"By who?"

"I don't know."

I burst into tears, feeling terribly hopeless. "What are we going to do? We're never going to get out of here!"

Aidan gently took my face in his hands. "It's going to be alright. We're going to get through this." He gave me a loving kiss, then the vehicle darkened when we fell beneath a shelf of thick smoke. The sounds of blasts and booms going off all around reverberated throughout the vehicle. I looked down to see flames integrated with smoke and the remains of blasted buildings. The vehicle touched the ground, then moved toward a clearing where I made out other vehicles parked in uniform vertical lines. Our vehicle stopped behind another, then the doors opened, causing me to cough and gasp for air.

"Breathe into your shirt." Aidan stretched the neck of my tank top up to my face covering my mouth and nose with the fabric.

"Put your hands behind your head and get out of the car!"

A taser gun pointed straight for Aidan's face was the first thing I saw, then the man holding it came into view. He was not dressed in black, didn't have a stoic expression and seemed to think that Aidan was the enemy.

"Get out of the damned car! If you try anything I'll shoot!"

Aidan held his hands behind his head, more than willing to comply.

"No!" I yelled, hugging his body close to mine. After everything we had been through, I wasn't about to let a misunderstanding ruin our chances of making a getaway.

"We're just trying to get home." I admitted, staring up into the man's blue eyes.

"I don't know what he's told you, Hon, but none of it's true. Now, get out machine!"

"I swear to you, he's with us!" I gasped, no longer caring that my lungs burned terribly.

"That's impossible."

"We're part of a community, that's where we're trying to get back to!"

The man didn't look convinced.

"He killed Geoff! I saw it with my own eyes! His own kind are after him!"

"That may be true, but I can't trust you."

"You have to!" I cried.

"How do I know you haven't been brainwashed?"

"Because..." Tears got the best of me again. "He's my lover!"

"What?" A puzzled frown appeared on his face and the gun lowered slightly.

"It's alright, Ivory," Aidan said, setting a foot outside of the vehicle.

"No!" I held him to the seat. "Please? Just let us go. There are others that need your help. There are buildings full of innocent civilians."

"We're working on getting them to safety right now. Everything is going to be okay, I just need you to come with me and we'll sort all of this out."

"We're not going anywhere." I stated, shaking with determination. I bore my eyes into the man's head. "I love this man and I would do anything for him. If you kill him, you kill me." I paused, silently pleading with my eyes. "We just want to go home, please? You can take all of his weapons and whatever else you want. We're both badly injured, all we want is to go in peace."

The gun lowered even further as the man appeared to be having an internal struggle.

"Please?"

"Just send her home." Aidan said, looking defeated. "I don't care what you do to me."

"Gavin?" A voice called from beyond the smoky haze. "Is everything okay over there?"

He looked from me, to Aidan, his eyes full of uncertainty, then something changed in them.

"Yeah!" he yelled back.

He stepped toward Aidan, still holding the taser firmly in one hand, then began removing what was left of Aidan's weapons from his vest. One by one they were tossed to the ground until every last one had been confiscated. He mumbled something beneath his breath then pressed the screen of a small device. The vehicle's doors closed and we were once again floating in mid-air.

"Check-in complete. Proceeding to destination OA-53."

Aidan's arms dropped as we breathed away all of the tension, staring into each other's eyes for what seemed like forever. We nestled into a loving embrace, warm and safe in a perfect cocoon. There was no need for words as we floated away into the sunset, completely forgetting about everything but the love we had for each other.

serenity

Big innocent eyes stared back at me as I scooped the last bit of apple mush from a jar. Fin's tiny hands slammed into the plastic tray before him, nearly knocking apple everywhere. I unloaded the spoon into his mouth getting a spray of puree in the face.

"Aaahhh!" he exclaimed, roaring loud and clear.

"You think that's funny, don't you?" I smiled, always enjoying time with my little buddy who'd grown to be quite a chunk.

A muted snicker turned my attention to the red-headed girl sitting beside me. Flora pursed her lips together, trying desperately not to laugh.

"So do you," I smirked.

"I just can't get over how adorable he is. He never seems to be aware of the fact that his face is covered in slop, yet he always manages to shower you in it."

"That's his favorite part of this whole experience."

We smiled at each other each.

"Here, you can feed him the last bite." I handed Flora the spoon and jar as she took my place, cautiously inching the spoon toward him. Fin happily accepted it, giving her a smile.

"He likes you," I grinned, taking my hair out of the ponytail it had been in all day. "All of the children do."

"I hope so. I'm still nervous about teaching on my own."

"Kia won't leave you alone until you're ready."

"I know, I just want to do everything right."

I smiled, glad to have my cherished friend back. "You're still going to come and help me in the gardens some days, right?"

"Of course."

The front door swung open as Kia walked in with a clear container full of baking flour, her hair tousled and splotched with white poufs.

"Is he finished?" She rushed to the kitchen and set the flour down getting back to her endless batches of rolls.

"Yes, and he ate every last drop, as always."

"Thanks, girls."

I eyed the kitchen, which was covered in baskets and containers full of fresh baked rolls for the community dinner.

"Do you need help?" I asked.

"No, I've only got two more batches left."

A rapid knock at the front door sounded just before Cara bounded in.

"Ivory! Flora! Come on! Everyone's already gathering at the lake. We have to go get the boys!"

Kia sent us out with as many containers of rolls as she could. Cara, Flora and I walked with arms full towards the lake in the warm afternoon sun. We went directly to the long buffet tables where Hydra, Deidra, Rayne and a few others were busy organizing and getting everything together. I deposited my rolls then took a quick scan of the few other dishes hoping for Rowen's famous fruit salad. I wasn't at all surprised to see Hydra digging in, her plate already half loaded. She was fully entitled to do as she pleased with not just one, but two babies well on their way. She gave me half a smile and a wink before getting back to her food.

The community dinner was a new tradition we'd started in an effort to celebrate our freedom and come together more as a family, especially since we'd grown in numbers. After Geoff's death, his city was completely destroyed, along with all of the remaining institutions. Oliver had run into hiding, while all of the children were taken in by communities, safe and secure in a loving atmosphere. Adult humans and machines had also been rescued from the city and set free to live as they desired. Most of Geoff's creations were destroyed, though some had been re-programmed. The humans were once again flourishing, taking back what was once theirs and learning to share with their machine counterparts.

"Do you think Cai is with them?" Flora mumbled, her eyes searching the area around us.

I grinned. "I don't know, why? You didn't flirt enough last night at the lake?"

"What?" Her cheeks flushed crimson. "I did not."

I laughed. "Yes, you did."

Cara, Flora and I wandered towards the far east side of the cabins where all of the new structures were being built. We poked and prodded each other along the way, playing silly games that only we understood. Clanks and thumps echoed through the air as men from the community were in action building cabins in every stage of development. Some were finishing up interiors, some were working on brand new foundations, but the majority were preoccupied with working on framing.

We passed several wooden skeletons where men of all shapes and sizes labored away. Lots of friendly faces stopped to greet us and as always I politely smiled and waved back, but there was one structure that unfailingly held my attention. The only pair of unusual blue-grey eyes smiled into mine, causing me to grin.

"There they are," Cara gasped. "And none of them are wearing shirts today."

Flora looked to the ground, her face sure to be bright red. "Maybe we should go back to the lake?"

I laughed. "It's alright, Flora."

"I know. It's just that it still seems so improper."

"Oh, Flora..." Cara teased. "Guess who's staring at you in all his improper glory?"

"Who?" She kept her eyes to the dirt.

"Cai."

"He is?" She brightened.

My eyes went back to Aidan who pounded one more nail into a joint before taking off the tan tool belt from around his waist. He gently set it aside then took a drink of water from a bottle. I scanned his perfect upper body, seeing skin that was smooth and unblemished. He was completely clear of any scars or wounds that had once covered most of his chest and arms. All of the marks had been easily erased, making me forget just how bad it had been six months ago.

Talon took a drink from Aidan's bottle then they laughed

about something that had been spoken. Cai focused hard on a piece of wood looking just as flushed as Flora. Oran and Shiloh were still hard at work, though I did see Oran glance Cara's way for more than just a couple of seconds. We were only a few steps away from the beams when Aidan walked out and took me in his arms.

"Hi," I chuckled, playfully tickling his hips. We laughed and squirmed around, eventually getting to a passionate kiss.

"How was Fin?" he asked, smiling into my eyes.

"Good. Flora helped me give him a bath."

He eyed my face and hair. "What did he cover you in today?"

"Apples."

"Mmm, I like apples." He attacked my neck with kisses until a spray of water hit us. I looked to see Talon water bottle in-hand with a sly smirk on his face.

"What?" he laughed, getting a rise out of our reactions. "It slipped."

Aidan darted for the closest bottle and squirted him back, starting an all out water fight. They chased each other around the beams, eventually making it out to the field. Flora, Cara and I burst out laughing at the unexpected entertainment.

"They've been doing this all day." Oran said, walking over to join us after putting on his shirt. Cai followed, greeting Flora who couldn't stop smiling.

"They're so silly!" Cara laughed.

Off in the field, Aidan took the lid off of his bottle and doused Talon with what was left. Once they realized they were both out of ammunition, they chuckled at each other and headed back our way. Aidan flashed me a quick grin, then looked back to his best friend who had him enthralled with words. I smiled, thinking they were lucky to have each other.

After we had arrived back home from the city, it took everyone a while to recover. Talon, Oran and Darius had been badly injured, while Rowen had managed to escape unharmed. Dryst had died instantly, causing lots of tears and heartache for many, though I was sure no one suffered over his death more than Aidan. The realization that he was in fact a machine, along with the hurt he had inflicted, caused a long period of suffering that was difficult for both of us. He eventually came around and returned to his old cheerful self, but I knew that deep down he would never truly forgive himself. Luckily, everyone else loved him and accepted him regardless of it all.

"Where's Phina?" Talon questioned as they joined us again.

"She's still cooking." Cara said. "You're supposed to go get her."

"You ready?" Talon asked, looking to Shiloh, Cai and Oran who were all fully clothed. Aidan slipped his shirt back on while Talon threw his over his shoulder.

"Yeah, let's go."

The group gathered and slowly began to saunter towards the lake. Aidan took my hand in his then smiled before pulling me in the opposite direction.

"What are you doing?" I smirked.

"I want to show you something."

Talon looked back at us, giving Aidan a knowing grin.

"We'll meet up with you later!"

"Okay."

Aidan led me into the wild forest. We trudged along a well-worn path that led to one of our many special spots.

"Where are we going?" I grinned.

"You'll see." His eyes darted from tree to tree, then he stopped us. "Alright, now close your eyes."

"What?"

"Close your eyes."

I did, dying to know what he was up to. It was somewhat difficult to walk over the rocky terrain but Aidan did a good job of keeping me from falling over myself. I held onto him until he stopped me and turned me slightly to the left.

"You can open them now."

My eyes fluttered open to see the framing of a medium sized cabin nestled in a small clearing amongst the trees. The creek that Aidan and I had dubbed our own gurgled a few feet away, as well as a cove of rocks we often visited. Despite the structure's towering beams and ample use of space, the area still had a feel of seclusion. I couldn't help but think how much it seemed to just belong right where it was.

"What is it?" I asked, thinking it must have been special to be away from the others.

"It's a cabin." Aidan smirked.

I playfully bumped him. "I can see that."

"Do you like it?"

"What is it for?"

"You."

"Me?" I looked to him in question. "What do you mean?"

"It's all yours. I need you to tell me how you want the inside designed so I can finish it."

I studied his face. "You're serious?"

He laughed. "Yes."

"You built this for us?"

"I thought it was time we moved into our own home."

Tears welled in my eyes as I threw my arms around him, elated by the fact we would actually have a home of our own. It had been a dream of mine since the new developments began.

"Really? It's really ours?"

He smiled. "Yes."

I squealed and gave him a big kiss, then bounced over toward the structure.

"Do you like where it is?" he asked. "I wanted it to be somewhere special."

"I love it! It's perfect."

We stepped onto the foundation where all of the main rooms had already been mapped out and excitedly plotted where we thought everything should go. It wasn't hard at all to imagine how it would look as flashes of the finished product and what it would feel like danced in my head. Any space that was Aidan's and mine was always magical. We took our time fantasizing, getting just a little carried away, then lay in our "bedroom" on the dirt we decided would be the spot for the bed. I rested my head on Aidan's chest as he cradled me in his arm.

"I want to hang our art on that wall." I pointed toward our feet. "And maybe some in the kitchen."

"Yeah, I thought I'd leave the decorating up to you." He paused. "Rowen insists it's a woman's job."

I smiled. "Really?"

"He got in trouble for having an opinion about the nursery."

I busted up laughing, finding Hydra's new condition and the personality that came with it amusing.

"Well, I'll let you have *some* say in it."

"You will?"

"Maybe."

He tackled me with tickles as we got lost in each other, completely unaware of how dirty we were getting. I broke one of many kisses, staring deep into his eyes.

"Thank you."

He nuzzled his nose into mine. "You're welcome. I would do anything for you."

"I know."

My ears picked up the sound of a little voice.

"Ivory! Aidan!"

Akela came bounding through the brush with a big happy smile, her hair tousled from a full day of play.

"Come on! Come on! There's sooo much food and it's sooo fun!" She twirled in a big circle, watching her dress poof from the movement.

Aidan and I smiled at each other before getting up to brush the dirt from our clothes. We made our way to Akela who bounced up and down.

"Do you like it?" She asked, looking up at me with her hands clasped together.

"You knew?"

"Yep!" She giggled, smiling at Aidan who took her in his arms.

"You are the best secret keeper ever." He said, taking my hand into his. "I'm going to keep all of my secrets with you."

She squealed with delight, then wrapped her arms around his neck before planting a kiss on his cheek.

"Thank you." He smiled, flushing ever so slightly.

"I love you just as much as Ivory loves you and I'm going to marry you someday."

I laughed.

"What about Hane?" He teased.

"He's nice, but he's not as strong as you are."

"I see."

I listened to Aidan and Akela carry on their enthralling conversation, then turned my attention toward the bright blue cloudless sky. I was grateful to be alive in a world where humans and machines co-existed in peace. It was only the beginning for all of us.

Melissa Kline

Melissa Kline penned her first novel at the age of thirteen and has been writing consistently for fifteen years. She has completed ten young adult novels and several short stories. Her preferred genre is young adult, but she writes non-fiction and children's books as well. Melissa's calling is to connect with others and give hope through writing.

She is a member of the Society of Children's Book Writers and Illustrators and founder of Rocky Mountain Women Writers, a Denver based writing group created to inspire women to write from their hearts and follow their dreams. Learn more at www.MelissaKlineAuthor.com.

Reading Group Questions and Topics for Discussion

1. How does Ivory develop as a character throughout the course of the novel?

2. Have you ever felt yourself confined by authority? How would you respond to that situation?

3. Ivory's differences are emphasized and she is identified as an outsider. What similarities do you recognize in your own peer environment?

4. In *My Beginning*, a plague killed nearly the entire human race. Can you think of a historic or even contemporary epidemic? Compare and contrast. How was it managed?

5. What threat is inherent in the relationship between males and females in the institution? How does the institution try to moderate that threat? Is it effective?

6. Imagine that you could only use one sentence a day to communicate with someone you're close to. What words would you use? How would the brevity change the quality of the conversation?

7. Ivory and Aidan were faced with risking their lives to escape the institution together. What would you risk to be with the person you care about?

8. Can you imagine what life would be like if you had to start all over? What is the closest experience you've had to being outside of what you are familiar with? In what ways were things different?

9. When Ivory and Aidan escape the institution they join a self-sustaining community that may be seen as utopian. Do you think that this book offers a model for a utopian society? What would your version of utopia be like?

10. If you were in a self-sustaining community what five foods would you cultivate to ensure your survival and how would you do it?

12. In *My Beginning*, the technology is so advanced that it is nearly impossible to tell the difference between humans and robots. What's the most sophisticated robot to date and how does that compare to modern technology?

13. How would you feel if you found out that someone you loved was not human? Would you still pursue that love? What are the risks involved with Ivory's affection for a non-human or machine?

14. What were antagonist Geoff Octavious Driscoll's motives? Compare his motivations and tactics with a contemporary or historical figurehead.

15. Geoff was surprised to learn that his machine developed the capacity to love. This suggests that love is more powerful than logic. Do you think this outcome is plausible?

Q&A with Melissa Kline

1. In the essay you published in the anthology *Speaking Your Truth*, you mention that you have written ten novels. Can you describe how your writing developed through this process?

    There is an evolution that occurs within every novel I write. Each and every one has taught me more about who I am as a person and a writer. My writing skills improve with every word.

2. *My Beginning* is your most recent novel and your first published fiction. How is it different from your previous books?

    "My Beginning" is the first science fiction novel that I have ever written. All of my previous novels are contemporary young adult.

3. How did you come up with the idea for this book?

    The plot for "My Beginning" came to me in a dream where I experienced Ivory's adventure firsthand. I was so taken by this mysterious world and knew upon awakening that it was something very special.

4. What qualities of Ivory's character do you relate with?

    Ivory's characteristics are very similar to mine. I relate most to her sensitivity, compassion, determination and courage.

5. Did people in your life inspire any of the secondary characters?

    Yes. Fin was inspired by my youngest son and Akela my oldest. Deidra and Hydra have the care-taking qualities of my mother, and Rowen's diplomatic skills are similar to my husband's. I have run into each "character" at some time or another.

6. How would you characterize the relationship between Ivory and Aidan? Are there qualities of this relationship that you idealize?

   Ivory and Aidan's relationship is one of unconditional love. I admire their friendship and the trust, respect and acceptance they have for one another.

7. In *Speaking Your Truth*, you also write that you escaped your own circumstances through writing fiction. Does your escape bear any resemblance to that of Ivory and Aidan's?

   Yes, very much so. I felt confined in many different ways as a child and have experienced a metamorphosis of change in my adult life that has set me free.

8. What experience in your own life inspired your representation of the community to which Ivory and Aidan escape?

   I left home at an early age and experienced the world through travel. I learned to be self-sufficient and depended on a community of friends for support. I also experienced the beauty of nature and how to appreciate little things.

9. Are there any side stories that you might develop further?

   Hydra and Rowen's story would be fun to explore. I'm also tempted to write about Geoff and his history.

10. Do you have an idea for a sequel?

    I'm toying around with a couple of ideas for a sequel. I've even thought of a prequel.

For *My Beginning* extras, visit
www.MelissaKlineAuthor.com

Extras include:
Miniatures
Props
Costumes
Interview with Ivory

Max and Menna
by Shauna Kelley

"*Max and Menna* is a heart-felt, heart-rending story of
abandoned children who must learn, as best they can,
to care for each other and themselves."

~Madison Smartt Bell, the author of twelve novels including *All Soul's
Rising*, a National Book Award and PEN/Faulkner Award finalist and
winner of the Anisfield-Wolf award for the best book of 1996 dealing
with matters of race.

Max and Menna tells the story of two siblings surviving a deplorable home
life in the South in the early 1980s. Telling the story from each of their
viewpoints, Max and Menna outline their reliance on each other and on
Nick, their only friend, as they cope with growing up in poverty, living with
an alcoholic mother, and having no indication of the other half of their
parentage.

The story opens with Max and Menna in the eighth grade. They meet
Nick, a Native American, and the story continues to take place during their
summer vacations progressively through high school.

Max, quiet and introspective, struggles to understand how to be the only
man in the house and protect a family that seems determined to destroy itself. Menna is quick-tempered and vivacious, and grows to love and view
Nick as a method of coping with a childhood that requires her to be very
adult.

Despite the strength of the bond the three of them share, however, their
environment works against them. As the children of the town drunk, the
younger siblings of the town slut, and the friends of an Indian from "over
the fence," Max and Menna fight not only to grow up, and get out, but to
stay together, and stay safe.

ISBN: 978-0-9844627-4-2
(Ages 15+, also available in hardcover and ebook formats)

9 780984 631759